Ting Tang Tales

Ting Tang Tales

(Part One)

by

D. R. Singh

Golden Antelope Press
Kirksville, Missouri
2008

ISBN: 0-9747968-9-1 (978-0-9747968-9-5)

Library of Congress Control Number: 2008928650

Published by:
Golden Antelope Press
715 E. McPherson
Kirksville, Missouri 63501

Available at:
Nitai's Bookstore
715 E. McPherson
Kirksville, Missouri, 63501
Phone: (660) 665-0273
http://www.nitaisbookstore.com
http://www.blazingsapphirepress.com
Email: neal@blazingsapphirepress.com

Contents

Introduction

I dedicate this book to my brother the bouquet Beans Rumpeltinskino who inspires me with his ready comedy, island coolness, philosophies and easy-going-ness.

I am a diasporic Indian bred in Trinidad, a British Caribbean island. I live in Puerto Rico and hardly get the chance to speak real English so I hope this book is understandable. I know that dialect is usually unintelligible, but it was used in my stories to create a bit of confusion and smiles.

My sister Mala encouraged me to write and Mr. Neal Delmonico helped with editing and general support. I'm grateful to my mind for being steady enough to complete everything, and my nice mountain home, full of peaceful inspiration.

I need to thank an unspecified curry antelope at this point. It's my wish that readers enjoy these exclusive fables that contain valuable lessons for one and all. Their beauty is that they are different and new. I never enjoyed peddling quail mangoes.

Some of the stories are true and some not. Some are recent and some set way back in time. Readers are allowed to determine which is which.

If a reader believes that a pig can drive a school bus and a blade of grass can learn to meditate and a coconut can dance, then it's nothing short of the truth! These things do exist as broad as daylight!

Believe it or not, there are playful dogs that can talk and hop backwards on two legs and ambitious cows that give powdered milk and dance the Macarena. You can't see everything. Some things you have to depend on others to see for you. That's why I'm standing here opening your eyes as to how exactly it happened.

The best way to enjoy something is to believe it. Have faith, as the pastor says. Faith is what moves the mighty mountain.

Whoever heard of a unisex pumpkin with brains that didn't work or a good for nothing turkey? Or jack-fruit that couldn't form their own committee? Not me for one!

I've personally seen people kneading bread dough with jigger feet and Indians sheltering from the rain with *dasheen* leaves. If not, why on earth would I be over here telling you about them? And a prime minister who hung from a mango tree and and and and ...

If you quiet doubting Thomas back there you'll even be able to speak and understand animal languages, and I'm not saying that English is not one of the most powerful animal tongues around. But I'm here talking about four-legged animal Latin.

All it takes is to believe, as the pastor says, and it shall be revealed unto you.

If you were not fortunate enough to have witnessed such events, then dear ladies, gentlemen, boys, this book is my gift to you.

A last piece of advice. If you want to get the most out of these narrations, I recommend you turn the book upside down and then start reading from the back. That's how I usually read my literature. You just understand better that way.

Till then dear readers, take care and good night.

Ting Tang Tales

The Healing Swami

A Fancy Guru

A fancy healer from India showed up in America to see what opportunities were in store for him. He set up shop on the West Coast and lay in wait. In India, he somehow had secured the title of doctor, but as he established himself in the West, he became known as a blend of yogi, swami, doctor, psychic, guru, or whatever was in vogue at the moment as far as the healing arts were concerned.

The "doc" based some of his conclusions on information derived from scanning through books like *Bhagavad Gītā*, where he learned about the three modes of material nature and so forth. So he put these ideas to work on his patients. They, of course, had good American names like James or Thomas. They were in awe of this mystical, spiritual healer from the Far East. So they flocked to his office for attention.

There were three patients who were distinct from each other and according to the understanding the doc weaned from the books, he mentally labeled them the good, the bad, and the heated. The good one stood for the mode of goodness, the heated for the mode of passion, and bad one for the mode of ignorance.

He showered them with sweet words and tried to balance off each one to make him function smoother. The good guy was a vegetarian who ate only fruits, milk, honey, and bread—his brain functioned quite well, his complexion was clear, and he was a peaceful man who had a liking for studies, meditation, and charity. He made a living by teaching, so all day long he was with the book.

However, his wife nagged him about being too 'cool.' He read constantly and would not move around. The pounds were creeping up and a round shape was taking possession of him. He went to visit the famous guru-doctor with the question: "Master, how can I be a little less cool?"

And the master answered and said unto him, "*Shanti! Shanti!* My child. Let not your heart be troubled. Why fear when Doctor Swami is here? You are nothing but cosmic energy—ever existing. This little worldly problem will go away with a small change in your diet. But focus on you—who you are. You are eternal light—share it with others. You are divinity. Meditate on who you are. Your wife may be indicating to you that you need to be more passionate. For the soul passing through this world, that is sometimes needed. Add hot spicy foods to your diet. That will do the trick. But meditate on you, the most important element behind this cosmic force."

The good one emerged from the swami's office in a state of levitation, for no one before had rated him with cosmic divinity. Now these were the types of words that drew in members of the peace and love gang. The swami, by observing their habits and physical forms was able to decide which of the categories they fitted and consulted them to suit. They came away with the impression that he had mystic powers. A very passionate-natured chap came in and the swami detected a restless halo.

" What ails you, my son? I see you are having a troubled time?"

"I believe I'm too restless, master. I am a workaholic. I cannot sit still to enjoy fine arts and music. I am always on the go. I have symptoms of stress and high blood pressure. I can't seem to gain an ounce of weight because of my constant bustling. I am even having extra-marital affairs because of my uncontrollable lust."

"Peace be unto you, *Om Shanti!*" answered the swami-doctor. "You seem to be controlled by the mode of passion and the cure for that is diet change. Do you eat foods that are hot, salty, sour, and spicy as well as a lot of meats?"

"Yes, those are what I mostly eat. They are my favorites."

"You must balance them with fruits, salads, and sweets. You see, my child," he looked away thoughtfully, "you are not a part of this illusionary world. Identification with this gross existence causes suffering. We do not belong to this physical sphere. Of course, you must also attend to bodily problems because the body is your temple. Use a multivitamin supplement. Valerian is good to keep you calm. Deep breathing for half an hour a day will tranquilize you, but the solution to your problems is meditation. Distract yourself from this tiny problem for a moment for you are a light—the very root of this cosmos. You are a tiny spark that makes up the complete God. You are God, so to speak. And God does not experience miseries. The soul that identifies with matter experiences pain. So tune in to who you are—and experience peace and bliss. You are none but the divine *shakti*—God himself."

The heated one could not believe his luck. The discovery

that he was God turned him into a lifetime meditator and worshiper of the guru, who had opened his eyes to this transcendental information. His diet was modified accordingly and he began to chant the mantra: *Ayem, Ayem, Ayem*, three sessions a day as taught by the healer. He felt his life taking a more peaceful turn.

The bad one, afflicted by the mode of ignorance, turned up at the guru's office.

"Master, I don't have to tell you of my situation. You have the vision to see everything."

"Blessings my son," replied the master. "It's not hard to see that you are attached to using drugs and alcohol. You sleep and laze about a lot and you prefer to eat stale foods and meats."

"It's a fact. I never cook fresh. I eat only frozen or fast meals and canned and preserved meats. I am always groggy headed and can out sleep a bear. I am not in shape as you can see. My flesh always seems to grow in the wrong direction," wailed the bad one.

"That is right. I can see right through you, that this food has settled in the wrong places. You do have a box like appearance. However, that is minor. Behind this undesirable appearance is a beautiful flame that burns through the layers of the universe to merge into the divine energy. You must contact that flame—and experience the divine whole of which you are the basis. Your diet should revolve around fresh fruit mainly. But more important in your life should be the meditation. Before the sun comes up, bathe and sit in the yoga posture and chant the *Om* mantra for an hour. After that you must do half an hour of yoga to bring your shape back to normal. Later on that must be increased to an hour."

"I know nothing of yoga, my dear guru."

"Here is a book with diagrams. You should do the Sūrya Namaskār and the deep breathing exercises. This combined with the diet and the mantra should take care of your problems."

The distinguished healer was known by the name of Anand Gupta. He was not an unattractive man. He had golden skin, dark glossy hair, and eyes which gave you the feeling that he was floating on a planet of bliss and wellness. He was of medium build with strong limbs and his voice was velvety soft.

He was also well read in the ayurvedic texts so he merged that knowledge into his curing business. He would explain at times that all diseases were based on a disturbance of the *Vata*, *Kapha*, and *Pitta* energies in the body. This meant all cures could be possible simply by balancing the flows of *vata*, a cold, dry energy, with *kapha*, which is cold and wet, and *pitta*, which is hot and oily. This was another technique that fascinated his western followers so much so that they began to grow upon him like leeches.

Using this format he divided his customers into three groups: the dry, the cold, and the hot. Some of his patients were combination types like dry and hot or cold and dry, and so on. Treatment as usual was diet adjustment, meditation, and yogic exercise.

A gangly, dry-looking guy with joints that crackled sailed into the office for consultation.

"You're suffering from an excess of *vata*," counseled the doctor without being asked. Wheat is beneficial for you to

8

keep you grounded. Don't eat anything with yeast. It will increase *vata*. You need a lot of cooked food which should be spiced with a lot of *asafoetida*. Sweet reduces *vata*, but do not use heated honey. It is poisonous"

A ball-shaped female with square shoulders and heavy calves rolled into his office. "You are a victim of *kapha*, " he explained. "Now we will get the ball a rolling by advising that you cut down on all grains. Eat all types of vegetables but potatoes and tomatoes and avoid sweets. Eat a lot of chillies and hot, pungent spices. Stimulants like black tea are good. Oils, nuts and legumes are not advisable for your type."

A sweating, *pitta*-driven man was next. He had coppery skin, pimples and rashes and some graying hair due to his excess heat. He wore short pants and an undershirt. The doctor advised him: "Give up the sour, salty, and pungent tastes and adopt the sweet, bitter, and astringent tastes"

"I know nothing about these things, Dr. Gupta," answered the confused man.

"There are six tastes," answered the doctor. "Sweet, sour, salty, pungent, bitter and astringent. You can read about them from this list which you can take home. Choose wisely and eat. A careful balance of these tastes in your every day diet will even out the malfunctioning *dosha*."

Curing the ayurvedic way was simple and impressive. He wrote books on yoga, diet, and meditation. He had twenty-five titles on the shelves. Now these revered scripts were glorified by people like the Lama and Larry King who called him on his show every six months to debate with religious and meditation heads.

He was called prophet by some. His book called *Real Love*

inspired a lady from Europe to "divorce her husband and live with her sheep on a farm," according to her testimony.

You see the doctor's method was simple: he doled out as many oriental terminologies and methodologies as he could manage to people who knew nothing of them. A sort of jack-of-all-trades but master-of-none he was.

He enticed customers with a maze of high-sounding, eastern jargon, weaving a spell over them like the spider who invited the little fly to walk into his parlor which was nothing but a webby trap.

In a curious effort to decipher what was taking place and a tremendous attempt to unravel things, his clients said mantras, did yoga, got high and rumbled out mystical eastern terms.

It must be told that most of his books carried titles like *Finding God, Ten Secrets of a Successful Life, The Path to Riches, Yoga and Meditation.* All these carried the identical message in a different form and jacket. But people accustomed to "judging a book by it's cover" bought the same message over and over.

For instance he had a book called *How to Get Rich.* Open this book and what would you find? Lo and behold, you would find the same cosmic divine soup spooned out with a different ladle: "Affluence is not about money, but the flow of riches from the universe. The riches that flow from your soul, being carefree, serenity, doing service, charity, meditation, cosmic divine bliss," and so on. "Understand your true nature as spiritual energy and health, relationships, and material abundance will flow." The identical message repeated in the other twenty-four books would be camouflaged once more in a new book.

This message was a personal twist of the teachings of various eastern holy books which any ninny could get hold of and read. Due to laziness and attraction to a pretty cover, ninnies were duped twenty-five times with the same bait.

Excerpts from holy books concerning attachment to this world and the "field of action" were put into his words and assembled into a book, bringing him further fame. By reading a verse each day, flashes of enlightenment would come from within, he promised.

He published books about prayers taken from the Dead Sea Scrolls, the Third Eye, the Secrets of King Tut, and the Wisdom of Moses, to show people that he was an all-rounder.

All his how-to books carried the same simple instructions only a dope would need to be told in these times, tossed with a *masala* blend of inspiring words for easy assimilation. A book on health tips would advise: get sleep, eat the right food, mind-body integration, eliminate toxins, encourage love, deep-breathing , exercise, vegetarianism, as if it was the first time this was being heard in the West.

Never mind the five thousand books that were already written on the topic based on the original Vedic or Buddhist texts. However, twenty-five more authored by him stormed the market and were devoured by a group of confused Confucians.

Now this group of confused Confucians spanned all the continents, for the doctor-swami propagated his teachings over the net and Dr. Gupta even believed in his own propaganda when he had the time.

And did he have the time to believe? Well certainly not. From dawn to twelve midnight he ran his Gupta empire from his offices in California. Did he perform charity? No one asked for it. No time to notice millions living on the streets of India.

Meditation? There was so much business starting at the sacred hour of three in the morning that there was not a minute to spare for that. Compassion for his countrymen who were less fortunate? No, no, the memory of their suffering had disappeared a long time ago, with the coming of his American fortune.

The message, with its twenty-five different titles and covers, had to be discussed, re-discussed and re-discussed on talk shows and peddled far and wide. The stress of the business was building toxins as fast as he tried to eliminate them. A word of acknowledgment to the masters whose books he had copied his ideas from? No, that would diminish his credit. Anand Gupta was guru of pop and movie stars, the highest spiritual authority and THE bridge over troubled waters.

His business was spinning money and he became the most wealthy swami of his time. Though he dished out yoga, meditation and *āyurveda* all day long, he himself hardly practiced any. His attachment to the worldly situation was more obvious than his patients', for he had left India with the aim of amassing, not shedding worldly acquisitions.

To the western eye, he was a master because of the judge-a-book-by-its-cover habit: his skin color, demeanor, and language. However, this cosmic connection which he preached day and night scarcely applied to him. His lifestyle lacked the things he taught. The master did not practice what he preached.

Now, as is inevitable, old age overpowered him and eventually his period of existence in that body came to an end.

12

He crossed over. His son took charge of the business. He was a more straight-forward man. He hired doctors to attend to clients and went about his father's book-selling business. He himself was not into the ethics that founded the business. His diet was regular and he drank and smoked. However, he was a charitable man who always had a soft spot for those not thriving too well.

He sent charity for the poor in India and Africa and never failed to give a few dollars to a beggar or homeless person. Therefore, God was always looking down at him with kind eyes, even though his habits were not perfect and he did not practice his father's teachings.

He had a business approach to everything. He wore his heart on his sleeve and no one was under illusion as to who he was. His habits were no secret and his honesty endeared him to all and sundry.

Twenty years had passed since his father's death. He used to be very kind to a young man who sold incense for a living. He would make sure to buy a dozen packages whenever the boy knocked, even though the Gupta Company was also a major distributor of incense in the US.

The boy would come once a week, never once to be turned away. He would sit in the air conditioned office to escape from the summer heat and they would chat as if they were old friends and even have iced tea or refreshments together. The boy struggled for money for his room and board, for he had been neglected by his parents who were both remarried. The head of this big company took compassion on him and even took some time off to converse with him though he was a nobody who worked endlessly to pay his room rent of five hundred dollars or else face homelessness.

"I like this place very much," the boy would say.

"It seems to like you also," the head of the company would answer and the boy would stay for an hour, wishing that he never had to leave. But then he would leave and continue knocking on doors and bleaching in the sun.

His strange, nostalgic attachment to that particular location was, as you may have guessed, because he was none other than Anand Gupta reincarnated. Mr. Gupta was a man devoid of personal religious practice and charity, in spite of all his preaching. In spite of the fact that he possessed such fortunes, he had made no real effort to connect to that divine cosmic energy he always dished out to others.

Therefore, his doom was to be recycled in the same material world that he always warned his clients about. This time he fell into destitution and loneliness. But thanks to the kindness of his former son, the boss of his company, a man with no fancy pretenses about himself, his present incarnation was not so unbearable after all.

Dr. Kook

"This is your favorite psychologist Dr. Kook, and I am getting ready to take your calls. Hello, you're on the air."

"Yes, good morning doctor. I believe I have a problem. I sometimes see lips moving but I don't hear no sound."

"Well you may be suffering from a disease called deafness."

"I didn't hear you."

"I said you might be hard of hearing."

"Could you speak up a little Doc?"

" You should try to get yourself a hearing aid."

"Doc, I'm sorry I can't ..."

SLAM!

"We have a caller on line two. Hello, you're on the air."

"Hello Doctor, thanks for taking my call. I get terrible leg pains after I go to the gym."

"Well, you just need to use some Bengay."

"But my wife won't give me any money."

"So use your own. You work, don't you?"

"Yes , but I'm in too much pain to go to the pharmacy, and I prefer to spend my wife's money whenever I have to."

"Then get your wife to go over and buy two tubes, because I'll need one for myself after I come over there and kick your ass."

"We go now to Crooksville. Hello, you're on the air."

"Good morning. I have a problem with my neighbor."

"What seems to be the trouble between you?"

"Well his dog comes over to my property and messes on my lawn. I find myself sliding in dog manure all the time. I've asked my neighbor to control his dog and keep it off my place, but he does nothing about it."

"And what part of Crooksville do you live?"

"108 Street."

"I'm extremely familiar with that area. Does your neighbor have a gray bushy mustache and a matching hairstyle?"

"He certainly has."

"Well you best get used to that slimy lawn, cause that's the same guy I see in my mirror every morning, and I ain't doing a damn thing about it."

"Hello, you're on the air with Dr Kook."

"Doctor, I'm a first-time caller and a first-time listener. My problem is my girlfriend. I'm want to take her home to meet my family, but I need help. It is impossible for me to do it by myself."

"And why is that so?"

"She is so heavy. I can't lift her up to put her in the car, and if I manage to, my car cannot take off with all her weight."

"Can't she go riding you piggyback style?"

"No, because the last time I tried it, they had to call an ambulance. I was nearly squashed to a pulp, and they had to rush me to the hospital to pump back life into me."

"Let me see if I can think of something. I don't know what else to say ... If nothing else works, try cutting her up into cubes to spread out the weight. In this way you can transport her bit by bit."

"I'll think about the idea, but I won't promise to do it. It sounds rather sick, I must say."

"I always say you must do what you must do. Is this our next caller? Hello, you're on the air with Dr. Kook."

"Good day, doctor. I'm a male Hezbollah who hates Jews."

"And why may I ask?"

"My mother was killed in a suicide bomb attack in their country, Israel."

"Were you there when the attack took place?"

"Yes, I sure was."

"And how did you manage to escape?"

"The suicide bomber happened to be my boyfriend and he had warned me about it before."

SLAM!

"Hello, next caller please, you're on the air."

"Good morning , Doctor Kook, I like your show very

much."

"Me two."

"Me three."

"So how can I help you today?"

"I would like to co-host your show because it seems you don't know a shit about a damn thing and you don't know how to treat callers."

SLAM!

"Good morning, line three, you're on the air."

"Hello, doctor, I have a death on my hands and I need your help."

"It's my pleasure to do whatever I can."

"Pleasure? My grandmother just had a heart attack from listening to your morbid barking, and I am planning to sue you for the cause of her death."

"And how much would you sue me for?"

"About a hundred dollars 'cause she was around a hundred."

"Okay, don't sweat now. I'll send you a check in the mail. Is that okay?"

"It sounds great to me. Thank you very much, doctor."

"Next caller please. You're on the air."

"Hello, doctor. My wife just threw me out of the house and filed for divorce, and now I have nowhere to live."

"I had the same problem about two years ago. Can't you rent a place?"

"Well I have been unemployed since Sept. 11."

"I think I have a solution for guys like you. I have a mobile cardboard box camp downtown, and I am renting it out at five dollars a month. You can pay whenever you get a job."

"But how can I live in such a place? I am the highfalutin' type, you know."

" Highfalutin' my ass. Where the hell do you think I live, scumbag? In this radio station ?"

"No."

"I give on-site training to my tenants and offer service with a smile. So don't waste time. I'll be waiting for you tonight."

"Okay. Let's go to line one. You're on the air."

"Doctor. My father is in his nineties and he still won't name me as the benefactor of his estate."

"And how old are you?"

"Sixty. I am his only child, and I need money to put down on a house."

"Ah I see. You don't have much time to play around with."

"Correct. I'm applying for a thirty year mortgage. What do you suggest?"

"If I was you I would call on Doctor Kevorkian to put him to sleep quietly, and then you will be the natural heir to his estate."

"I will do just that. Thank you for your valuable advice, doctor."

"Let's go to our last caller. Hello, you're on the air."

"This is the station manager, and I have to terminate our contract over the air."

"What do you mean?"

"Do you see those two police officers closing in on you?"

"Yes"

"Well I sent them over to give you the best licking you ever tasted in your life,

after which you will be arrested and charged with enough offenses to put you away for a long time."

"I don't understand. Don't you realize I am a qualified psychologist? The show is packed with callers. What else do you want?"

S L A M!

Wham! Wham! Clobber! Clop! Slap!

"Please get me off the air!"

"On or off, it's time to face the music, tomfool!"

SLAP! KICK!

Kassava Davis

Kassava Davis

Kassava Davis was a government worker who was always on time for his job. In fact he used to set out for work before dawn. His wife used to wake up at four A.M. and prepare bake, a thick bread made of baking powder, margarine, and white flour. His daily lunch menu was either bake and *buljol*, or bake and cheese.

A thin slice of cheese was the filling for the bake. At least it smelled cheesy enough to cause an appetite, although the sandwich was so dry it required a Pepsi to wash it down, or else the eater would be choked in the process.

Kassava was a prim and proper man. He wore a white shirt, black garbardine pants and glasses with black frames. His job setting was the government treasury—in a cave of dusty files which may have been a hundred years old. Kassava was the caretaker of this stockroom of papers, while his wife scrimped and budgeted so that they could one day enjoy a luxurious lifestyle.

She controlled every cent of his salary and gave Kassava just enough money for his bus ticket and the lunch Pepsi. Kassava was quite pleased with the arrangement.

It must be noted that he was not fond of cassava in any

form, even as bread or pone. He was a bake man. He never drove nor wasted money on keeping a car. All his travels were made on foot or by the bus.

His wife prettied up the house with lace curtains with large frills which blew all over Kassava when he walked through. His wife bought a new divan set and put it in front of the TV. The plastic remained over the chairs just as they came from the store and a large throw went on top of it to keep the plastic from getting too old. Kasava did not protest a bit.

"Dear, I need you to paint the dining set for Christmas," his wife requested. Every year the set was painted a new color and it was Kassava's duty to do it. Then a plastic printed with apples, grapes and wine bottles was spread on the table, where the Christmas meals were eaten. The setting remained like this for the rest of the year.

Kassava's wife bought ham for Christmas and she would not even let the smell of it go to waste. It was the only time of the year when Kassava got a break from the bake/*buljol* — bake/cheese routine. Of course she was bound to send pieces of ham for Nennen, Tanti and Macomere and a few slices were kept to put in Kassava's bake, which the proud man shared with his co-workers. When the ham was scraped clean to the bone, it was then used to flavor a soup made with yam, *dasheen* and *eddoes* and the bone would be sucked, sucked and sucked, then recycled to the dog-plate for more sucking.

Kassava's nephew, Anton, who lived in the US, sent him a boom box. A special shelf was constructed for it high on the wall, in a place where anyone who walked into the room could spot it at first glance.

One day his wife made some cassava bread and he

expressed his displeasure. "I don't like anything made of cassava. I like *cou cou*. I don't mind corn dumpling but not this cassava thing, man." So she had to change the menu and and make *cou cou*. This was dinner of course, for he already had bake as usual for lunch at work.

She pressed her hair with a hot comb and put curlers to set it at night if she needed to look special. They were a very harmonious couple. On Saturdays she did extra cleaning and scrubbing and played the radio loud, and washed clothes and hanged them out. Sunday was ironing day and the meal of the week was cooked. So he had to set out early for the 'fowl shop,' choose a live chicken and have it killed and plucked. Then he had to 'make market,' buying lettuce, tomatoes, carrots, sweet potatoes, watercress, anything necessary for the Sunday salad, for it was the only day a salad was eaten.

If there was *dasheen* bush he would buy it for *callaloo*. Then she would make very tasty *pelao*, salad, *chow mein*, boiled plantains, stew, *callaloo*. She would cook up a storm, plus she would make iced grapefruit juice, from canned juice of course, although the fruit grew freely everywhere. But drinking the canned version made her feel more civilized.

After the cooking was done and the table was set, she would call, "Dear, come and eat. I take out food already." Kassava would appear and sit before the table. It was the only day he ate with knife and fork. His plate was placed on a table mat and his grapefruit juice was served in a floral glass with ice cubes which caused the outside to frost.

"Maybe we should buy straws," he suggested.

"Nah, we can't get so fancy. That is only for when you drinking from a bottle," she answered. She was learning eating etiquette from TV shows and newspaper articles.

"We need some napkins, though, so you could wipe your mouth when you eating." During the week he bought some so that he could start practicing the technique and his wife put them out on a napkin holder. Next time they took a meal together, she showed him how to do it.

"See that grease on your lips?"

"No, I don't see it."

"Well then feel it."

"I can't even do that."

"One thing about this eating business is you must always be conscious if there is food on your mouth. Otherwise we would never be able to eat in public, you know. I feel the best way is to imagine there is always something."

"I follow," he answered. And she showed him. After every two bites he took a napkin and patted imaginary soil on his lips.

"You must learn to eat better with knife and fork," she said.

"Is hard to eat without touching the food," he replied.

"Everything takes practice."

So he tried to improve his knife and fork skills and took almost an hour to slice off the meat from a big bone, which kept slipping away. After that he was about to pick up the bone to suck, when she saw him and shouted: " No, no, no. It's not proper to do that. You must leave out that part."

"OK."

"Now I will show you how to eat rice with a fork.

Sometime in Chinese restaurants they don't give you spoon, just chopstick. But you could use the fork to practice."

"OK, lemme try it ... but the rice dropping through the fork."

"Is OK, you must be satisfied to eat small delicate amounts sometimes. It does look more modern than when you have your cheeks full and you chewing, especially if you talking too. Don't worry about what fall through the fork. It falling back in the plate and so it will take longer to finish the food and that's good. You see, these days you can't gobble down food like a dog when you in public. You have to be slow, dainty and elegant."

"Is not so easy, man. I see why them Indian people does wipe up everything with their hand."

"I know, Kassava, but we is not Indian. We follow the English way."

"You mean I can't even eat cake with me hand?"

"No, cake is eaten with a fork."

"Well, look at my crosses. I don't mind learning, though. We might have to eat in public one day."

By the time he was finished with his lessons, he was so fed up that he treasured the bake and cheese sandwich alone at the office, only because she wasn't there to supervise him.

One evening just as he came in his wife shouted: "Boy, you know Anton write and send a picture today. Look it here. Watch the dining set, nah. Is a big wood set with six chairs and is varnish they use, not paint. Oh ho, so that is how it is over there," she mused, admiring the picture, and showed it to him.

"Is nice. We does see sets like that on TV," he said.

When he settled down after eating dinner, she brought up the topic again. "You know, I think we should take out one of these sets. I see something similar in Ramsaran furniture store. We could take it on credit and pay monthly installments."

So they went and bought the set with six chairs and the old one was replaced. She made it look like Anton's as much as possible, with a fancy candle holder and a vase of silk flowers.

Then they invited Macomere and Tanti and Nennen and their husbands to eat.

"Like all you turn American, *oui*. I can't eat with this knife and fork and things," said Macomere.

"At least try, nah. I want to take out a picture and send it to Anton."

So Tanti, Nennen and Macomere struggled with knives and forks, while the more expert Kassava smiled at their efforts, and the photo was taken and sent to Anton.

One day, Kassava got called to jury service and his wife got out his suit and tie to prepare. She was going to put it in the sun, then iron it.

"But it's too hot for jacket, man. It's July you know."

"How could you go to court without a suit? The judge might boof you and also it won't look decent." Then she shined his shoes with Oxford shoe polish and he appeared a modern civilized man in court.

Kassava turned sixty and decided to retire early and live on a pension. He had savings stashed away and a desire to see America began to devour him and his wife. So the savings was put to use. His wife wanted to see how Anton was making out in America. Kassava wore the jury suit for the trip and Anton collected them at the airport and brought them to his home. Mrs. Davis immediately was stunned at the quality of everything and couldn't help touching and feeling every object as soon as she entered the house.

"But the set we bought at Ramsaran is different from this. This is the real thing, man. Look how solid. You could see this thing make in a factory. Ramsaran's furniture made and varnished by hand. Well, we get ripped off, but what you expect in Trinidad? To get nice factory made things like this? Kassava, I telling you a long time we shoulda leave that place. Look at the nice nice groceries. Everything in cans and boxes."

"Actually," said Anton, I miss the natural Trinidad mangoes and guavas ... "

"You crazy, boy? Pears, apples, tomatoes, already peeled in a can! ... Trinidad vegetables can't beat this! Imagine pre-washed lettuce. This is life , boy."

"But it ain't have no taste, aunty."

"So what you think sauce and dressing make for? For looks? It make to give food taste, boy. *YOU* have to make food look and taste good. Taste is not a problem, man."

And Mrs. Davis took the tasteless canned food and seasoned it with all the canned sauces she could find to make it delectable and they ate it with knives and forks and had store bought cake and ice cream for dessert.

"I miss the homemade coconut ice cream mammy used to make," said Anton.

"Well I find this better. You know I find the artificial

cherry tasting better than the natural one and the ice cream here ain't melting as fast as the Trinidad one, ain't it Kassava?" And Kassava had to agree, for he had now lost the power to disagree, but he reminded her that the cherries at home were Governor Cherry and Sour Cherry.

When they returned to Trinidad, Mrs. Davis could not help commenting at every waking moment how bad everything was.

"De damn road full of potholes ... In America the road and cars big and wide. You sitting in a car and you feel like you riding a plane."

"Well thank god I don't drive. We taking the bus to go all about," he said.

"You know Kassava, that is the same kinda backwardness I talking about. I think is high time you learn to drive, 'cause I getting damn fed up of this bus jucking me up. I getting too old for it man. You have to realize I ain't young no more, you know."

"Who say you young? It ain't so hard to tell," and the answer caused her to send him a pair of evil eyes, which made him retract. "It hard to tell, yes. If your knees didn't creak so much, I woulda mistake you for twenty-five."

"And who is the cause? I wanted to buy the Arnica cream in Florida and you make me forget. All I have over here is Vicks. You expect Vicks to stop creaking bones? All I getting here is suffering, yes. Not even a medicine for creaking bones."

"What about WD40?"

"Look man, they might look like steel but they ain't steel, OK? Go and rub WD 40 on you mother," said the woman now becoming mad.

So she constantly nagged him that her needs and wants could only be fulfilled by moving to America and they made the inevitable step towards it. He rented out the house expecting that the money would help to pay his expenses in the US.

On arriving there, Anton suggested that they find an apartment since his girlfriend had just moved in with two kids from another relationship and they would not have the privacy they were used to if there was family around.

So Kassava took his little savings and paid down a month's deposit and a month's rent on a small apartment and they began their dream life in America. Meeting expenses was beginning to seem a nightmare, when the wife hit on a plan to go to work. Kassava could not find a job because he did not have a work permit and he was too old to be hired.

"Don't worry, we go make it man. By the grace of God," suddenly she became a little god-conscious. And the woman with creaking knees contracted a job as house-cleaner for some Jews who paid okay, eighty dollars a day, and she took to work for the first time in her life. The first thing that she bought was a tube of Arnica and the creaking went away overnight, according to her.

The money they received from the house they rented back home seemed only a pittance against the grand amount of expenses. After the money was wired by Western Union to them, it was twenty dollars less, for Western is known to impoverish poor immigrants who want to send money back home, or receive money. The money helped pay the rent, but only a quarter of it. The rest was at least four hundred dollars.

But Mrs Davis was strong and she was determined that everything would work out.

She saved a little money and was able to furnish the flat with fine chairs, a dining set, bed, closets and all the other fineries and accessories she had seen at Anton's, and the table was always set with lovely crystal, lace, cutlery, and store-bought flowers in a vase.

"You see, here you don't even have to grow flowers. Everything on the supermarket shelf. I don't know why I waste so much time in Trinidad," she said.

So Kassava became a house-husband for a while and it was good for he had worked all his life. He did the shopping, cooking and cleaning and things went as smooth as any immigrant could have it. He tried looking for work but no one would take him without work permit and of course he did not have the credentials to become an undocumented house-cleaner, but his wife could not care less.

She was having a great time enjoying all the frozen dinners and cooked meals purchased at the supermarket, which were eaten with knives, spoons, and forks, and she held get-togethers with her new friends who were Caribbean immigrants, Americans and Cubans. The bake and *buljol* suddenly disappeared from their lives. She did not even have to get her clothes made by seamstress for here she bought all her dresses at Sears and Macy's, and even from catalogs.

But as you know people get weaker with age and the arthritis started to make her knees stiffer. The Arnica was becoming less potent. Before, it used to stop the creaking, but now a rusty sound was added to the existing creak that was now accompanied by stiffness. She had to buy Arnica by the case, for a tube lasted only a few days and did not have much effect. Still, she had to go do her master's work cause it was their only means of survival. Her friends recommended that she go see an arthritis specialist and she had to call a taxi to take her to the appointment since she could not even walk to the bus station. Why did Kassava not have a car and his driver's license at this point? No one knows. But it's one of the reasons that the story reached its climax.

"You see Mrs. Davis, the problem you have is caused by the food you eat and it's essential that you change your diet," the doctor observed.

"Well, is my husband Kassava who cooks and ..."

"Kassava? But dear lady just to start, that is one of the foods you should be eating. Also, I forbid you to eat anything that is not cooked at home."

"Well, so far, he is the one who made me sick with his food." The blame was dropped on him.

So, following the doctor's orders she had Kassava overhaul the menu drastically and he had to cook cassava twice a week. All the pre-cooked foods disappeared from the menu and surprise, Kassava even learned to make bake and buljol. His wife ate it for lunch at the Jew's home.

Still the knees did not improve much and the doctor then blamed it on age, for he could not use the humidity excuse. Everyone knows that Miami is as hot and dry as an oven, particularly during summer.

"Since you are already over sixty, there is not much I can do for you except prescribe drugs which will hide the symptoms of stiffness and pain."

So she had to take these drugs everyday before she went out because she had to bend and scrub the Jews' bathroom whenever they needed it to look shiny.

A year passed and she kept up the diet and drugs. She could not even dance for the Christmas and New Year's Party. She tried dancing but her knees remained stiff like a moko jumby and Anton's step-kids had a roaring time laughing at her.

"Well boy, Kassava, I can't eat, I can't dance, neither can I function without taking this drug every day and is real hard to be the only breadwinner in the family."

"To know it you must taste it. It wasn't so difficult for me because I was young," Kassava said.

"Is hard to enjoy life if you ain't healthy," she said.

She brain-stormed another plan. It was that Kassava learn to drive. She bought a cheap, used car for him. At least now he dropped her off and picked her up from work, and it made life a lot more easy. "I can't imagine why I didn't think of this before," she said.

"Me too," answered Kassava untruthfully. He had thought of it but was afraid of the idea since he had no experience. It was a pleasant shock to find out that most of the drivers in that area were over sixty and he was doing a better job than most of them. In fact most of the time he had to drive below the speed limit to run with traffic. His wife was delighted that he was driving slow and not like the "road hogs" back in Trinidad.

One day, the situation backfired when an eighty year old driver lost control of his car and hit them. They narrowly escaped physical damage, but the whole front of the car needed to be repaired and the job would take a few weeks.

"You know you try to solve one problem and a next one does come up. Where am I going to get money to repair it now?" she said. But the old man's insurance paid for the job although the car had to remain in the garage for a whole month while they went everywhere by foot or bus.

"You know, Kassava, I don't remember suffering so much in Trinidad." she said.

"You ready to go back?"

"I don't think is a bad idea. If things continue this way maybe we should move back in truth, oui."

So back they moved, but she visited the doctor for the last time before leaving. "Make sure you eat all those nice tropical fruits and vegetables. I think you should do some gardening, too. It's good to keep you active so that the arthritis won't affect you so much and the climate is better for you," he said.

Once home, she planted a nice flower garden which was the envy of her neighbors, and she even had plenty of flowers to decorate the vases in the house, where Tanti, Nennen, Macomere, and neighbors were constantly coming over, eager to hear about life in America. But she did not force them against their wishes to eat with knives, forks and spoons at the table. She tolerated that they ate with spoons alone, or however it was comfortable for them, once they did not eat like hungry savages.

"It ain't easy dey, boy. I won't recommend migration for nobody my age, nah. If you going dey to work you must be young and healthy."

"But you was healthy when you left here," Macomere said.

" I believe is all dem white people food that get she sick," said Kassava coming out of the kitchen with bake and *buljol* spillling out of his hand.

"At least sit down and eat nah man. You could eat that with a knife and fork," she almost slipped back into the old line.

"Look, leave me alone, *oui,*" Kassava shouted.

She made him drive and cook and they lived on his pension. She did not have to work and just planted her garden when she did not have friends over. Or, she went to the beach or to church.

And Tanti, Nennen and Macomere came around whenever there was a spare moment to hear about the fascinating life in America, far away from the little Caribbean island. Kassava and his wife even threw in some American slangs and accents to juice up the talks, and word spread about the wonders of this couple who had lived overseas.

One day Kassava announced: "I have to bathe and dress quick."

"Where off to?" his wife asked.

"Well each time I get invited to Ramkissoon prayers, I does turn it down. So I say let me go this time."

"You mean Hindu prayers?"

"Well I ain't going for the prayers. I just going in time for the food at the end."

"But you know they will make you eat with your hand."

"And? That is exactly what I plan to do. How long do you think you will rule me? Look, I enjoy bake and buljol with my bare hands and I want to try it with paratha, too. I will not eat paratha and curry with a fork," he shouted.

"You planning to make me ashamed or what?"

"Look lady, all my life I living to please you. From today, I live to please Kassava Davis. So live and let live."

And so Kassava finally came on his own, a bit late in life, but better late than never.

Jasso Maami

Jasso Maami was a glamorous dresser. She appeared or tried hard to be bubbly and joyful, but it was obvious that something was eating away her soul. Her dresses were fine, seamstress-made-to-order designs with brocades, appliques and sequins. She always wore matching *orhni* which was held on the shoulder with a jeweled brooch, while the veil was pinned to the head with black hair clips.

Her hair was always elaborately done—groomed with coconut oil, divided in the middle and formed into two plaits. Each of those was snaked around to create two *jooras*. This hairdo was covered with the veil or *orhni*, a transparent piece studded with sequins or other embellishments.

Apart from that, she was a walking gold mine—large *jhulani* earrings, intricate *hasuli*, *churiya* or bangles. She even had gold capped teeth. Her shoes were black pumps which tock tocked importantly.

Red lipstick and face powder always brightened her face which beamed with a loving smile, although you could never miss the hint of sadness behind it all.

Though she was a woman drowning in sorrow, she maintained this image of wealth and joy, specially when she visited her niece-in-law, Mani, in Rio Claro when she went there on business. Land business to be exact. Maami had seen some prosperous days when she was living with Rooplal who was Mani's maternal uncle. They were a married couple and had a little shop and owned five acres of land. Things were going very well, until Roop ran off with a beautiful damsel and that was the end of Maami's paradise. She was left to tend three kids alone and so she made the move of going back to Caroni where her blood family lived.

Maami rented out the land and came every month to collect rent. After finishing she would spend the evening with her niece-in-law and her children. It was easy to tell when she came. She would call out "Aye, *gyul*, I reach," and gave big kisses to everyone present, leaving moist red blobs on their cheeks.

She would feel at home as usual and sit down.

"*Gyul*, them renters want to rob me."

"How Maami?" asked Mani. Maami means wife of the maternal uncle.

"I went by all of them, Chunilal, Doon, Chabinath, and Sookraj and all of them wife say they not home. They tell me they gone to work. I wait, wait for them to come.

Then I say let me go, I go come back next month. You know as I was leaving I catch Chunilal hiding behind the house. When I ask him for the money he say he ain't working these days."

"I did tell you not to rent it out Maami," answered Mani.

"What I go do, *gyul*? Your *maamu* was not there to help me at the time. Chunilal them say they only putting up carat shack and nothing more. I say OK. Anything happen I could always get police to break it down. Next thing you know they build big big house."

"And how much rent they paying, Maami?" asked Mani.

"Paying? They promise to pay forty dollars a year, but up to now I only collect for the first two years and I hear that Sookraj making big big money."

"Is true. I really hear so," confirmed Mani.

"Yes, but he drinking too much. I can't find him sober at all," said Maami shaking her head in disappointment.

"Eat something, Maami," her niece- in-law offered in a comforting mood.

A plate of hot rice, *dal* and *chataigne tarkari*, freshly cooked on the *chulha*, was served. Maami sat and ate with hunger. She was squatting on the floor and scooping up the food with her hands, although there was an eating table right next to them. Mani also had the habit of eating like this.

She enjoyed the *chulha*-cooked food and Mani gave her tasty hot pickle to go with it.

After she drank water to cool down and washed her hands, she soon enough began her lamentations once more.

"Child the things your *maamu* do to me. He leave me alone with them children. I have to cut cane to feed them."

"I didn't know you was cutting cane, Maami," said Mani.

"Yeah, that is the work me family does do. They pay good, ten dollars a ton, and I finish work early. But I does have to go early morning, eh. By four o' clock I done reach the field. I does carry me food too. By ten o' clock I done me task and ready to go home," she explained.

"You working too hard, Maami," said Mani.

"Hard work good, child; it keep you bones strong."

Maami found someone to whom she could release her sorrow and tears appeared in her eyes. The veil fell from her head.

Mani's eyes also flooded with tears to hear of her aunt's plight.

"Make tea, Maami?"

"No, *gyul*. I have to take the bus now. The last bus leave at four o' clock. I have to go home and see about the children," said Maami. She put on her tock tock shoes, clipped up her veil, picked up her black purse that had the kind of lock that clacked, kissed everyone, and left. Once a month she came around to collect rent and each time a similar or identical scene played out.

The next month she was back. "Gyul, Chunilal, Sookraj, Doon and Chabinath is pure scamps. To cheat a poor lady like me."

"You didn't get to talk to them, even?" asked Mani.

"No, *gyul*, their wife making excuse, telling me they trying to make money to pay me. That they working barely to buy goods to cook."

"Have patience," said Mani. "God is with you."

On one of her trips Jasso brought a sister called Phoolbassia who was the center of amusement for Mani's kids.

After going about business, they landed at Mani's as usual.

"I bring me sister Phoolbassia for a outing," she introduced. In no time the two of them were eating hot delicious rice and *dal* with gusto.

Phoolbassia was a humorous sight. She had wide hips and bottom which stood apart and the feet turned inwards a bit. She looked like Huey duck and spoke in a low grating voice.

It was her first trip to Rio Claro and she and Jasso wanted to overnight at Mani's.

Phoolbassia quacked and quacked all night. "You have nice bed. Where you get them?" she asked.

"Me husband buy them when we first get married," answered Mani.

"Nice. And how you does polish the brass on the bed-bars?"

"I use brasso. I buy it in Lucien shop," said Mani.

"The teaster nice too. You make it?"

"Yes," said Mani. "I sew all," said Mani.

All night long she kept quacking and the children could not sleep listening to the Phoolbassia duck. By one A.M. she had not removed her gold necklace and *jhoomka*, because she was not ready to sleep. She kept going on all night while the respectful Mani kept answering all her questions with the fullest patience even though she was quite tired.

Next morning they left on the first bus with hot coffee in their stomachs.

The following months Maami came for her rent and

dropped in to see Mani as usual.

One time she began singing a different song. "I going to church now;" she was in a peaceful and sweet mood.

"Which church?" asked Mani.

"The church of Nazarene. Your *maamu* not there to help me so the pasta come home and invite us to come and he sending a van every Sunday for me and the children to go," Maami said.

"That good. I glad you getting help," said Mani.

"*Gyul*, Christ is with us and don't mind what you *maamu* do. I forgive him, and wish him well."

Mani nodded her head giving her best support as usual.

"The pasta want me to christen. He want me to born again. I thinking about it. If you see how they helping the children — school books, clothes. We don't have to buy nothing. The pasta say just come, surrender to Christ and we will get everything and go to heaven too. So I think is a good thing."

"That good," said Mani who had a lot of sympathy for Christianity as well.

"Christ forgive your *maamu* and I also forgive him." Deep down she still loved Rooplal and bore no trace of vengeance or hatred for him. "I hear he have eight children. I don't know how he supporting them. God feeding mine, I know that for sure."

Mani nodded to agree. At least the pastor succeeded in reducing some of her material miseries, an important factor for any kind of progress, Mani thought.

Maami gave up her Indian *bhajans* and said "hallelujah," "amen" and "praise God" whenever hymns were sung in the church, because she couldn't read English to follow the words of the hymns.

And she lived till the end with the firm faith that she had secured a place in heaven, because all saints who carried a cross of suffering in this world earned a place there. Its not sure whether the pastor had the power to ensure her passage to heaven, where she could walk the streets of gold, but at least he gave her a hope to live for and replaced her hopelessness.

The lipstick, powder and fancy clothes disappeared and she became a plain undecorated dresser, praising the name of Christ everywhere.

This is a true tale—one of suffering and hope. A tale of Jasso Maami, a legendary lady, a single mother who cut cane to put food in her children's mouths.

The Counted Avocados

"Good morning, Ramon," the old man knocked on his neighbor's front door, early one morning.

"Morning," answered the neighbor.

"I brought you a hand of green bananas. I had to pick a few bunches this morning. They are getting too heavy for the trees now. So I figure it's time I picked them and put them to ripe."

"Thank you very much," said the neighbor. "You are the most generous man in these parts," he flattered.

"People complain about me, but I am the most free-handed man in this village." It helped him to say it, but as the dictum goes, the desire for credit is in itself vulgar. But how can we accuse a seventy five year old man, who worked all his life, of being vulgar? --- We must not take that liberty at this point, but perhaps later on.

The old man had owned twelve acres of land. He had purchased it at fifty dollars an acre in the nineteen fifties. He divided six among his sons and kept the other six for himself. He kept it under crops: plantains, bananas, breadfruit, avocados, lemons, cilantro; whatever could come up was grown.

Day and night he kept an eagle eye on the property. The gift to Ramon was rare and maybe was made to lessen the burden of the load of bananas he was carrying back home that morning.

"I have to leave rapido," he said. "I must check on the avocados. My son is still in bed and he won't make his rounds until later." He left as swiftly as an old man could.

The son was a fifty-year-old semi-mute laggard, who was incapable of doing anything but supervised farm work. On the way home the old man counted the avocados. One, two, three, four ... There were twelve on that particular tree. They needed time to get full, so he left them alone.

Next morning, he dropped in around ten o' clock to see Ramon, who lived as a tenant in one of his houses.

"Did you hear noises around here last night?" he asked.

"Not a sound," answered his tenant.

"It seems," he said in worried tone, "that someone is stealing the avocados. Yesterday I counted twelve and today I saw only eleven." The old man was playing dead to catch *corbeau* alive.

The tenant got the jitters thinking that he must be the suspect.

"Well, I don't understand how someone would come to steal only one avocado," his tied tongue tried to juggle up something.

The old man left and could be heard yelling to his son in the distance, "Jose, go right now and count over the avocados. Look in the grass to see if any has fallen down. I am missing one!"

Jose came and began looking as if he was searching for a snake in the bush. He went back home. "No, pappy, I saw nothing on the ground. But all the twelve are on the tree. I just saw them."

"Blind foolish boy," the old man lambasted the retard. "You better drink some coffee and wake up. I personally counted eleven and you will stand there and tell me that you saw twelve!" He was quite upset by now.

The renter was an immigrant from the Dominican Republic who had come to better his position, but he could not afford to buy a house as yet.

"I was thinking," he said, one morning as the old man came by, "to buy a piece of land and put up a house on it little by little. Would you think of selling a quarter acre to me?"

"Well I never really thought of selling. You see, I bought land when it was very, very cheap. But that was way back then."

"How much did you pay?" the tenant ventured with a timid braveness and the old man gave him the ask-no-question-you-will-be-told-no-lies look, while trying to abort the loaded question.

"Everything has gone up now," he said. "This small lot you see here alone is worth thirty thousand dollars, but I have no plans to sell my land. I worked very, very hard for all this."

So the renter resigned himself to continue eating the crumbs that the old man spread on the table, until God blessed him with his own house and land.

The old man dropped by most mornings while making his

farm rounds. He had cows grazing in the field but would not spend money on a shed for them to shelter in when it rained. Violent rainstorms and hurricanes would brutalize them for days, and they would stand shivering in the furious weather. The old man thought only of the day he would sell them. This morning he carried an old bath tub.

"See what I got for the cows!" he called out. "It's for them to drink from. You must treat the animals right for them to develop healthy to the right size! ... I, for one, give my animals the best treatment possible," he shouted.

On his way back, he counted the avocados once more. Only eleven, he thought, and he cursed the wretched thief who took the missing one.

When he dropped in for his morning chat the next day, the tenant again asked him about property.

"How much do you suppose a house like this would cost?" The structure was an unfinished dwelling into which water from the hills above drained.

"A house in this state," replied the old philistine, "would cost you eighty thousand dollars, and that is without the land. Everything has gone up these days. Government wants you to pay so much tax on your property."

"How much do you pay?"

"You won't believe it. One hundred and fifty every year," he cried out. "Where will a poor man like me get that kind of money? This government is murdering poor people like me and you, Ramon. No one cares for us the down-trodden people of this country."

On the way back, he counted the avocados, and picked two that were ready for ripening.

In order to divert the water from draining into his home, the tenant paid one hundred dollars to someone with a backhoe to dig a drain to direct the water to the side of the house. Next morning bright and early the old man and his son set to work filling up the trench the tenant had paid to have dug.

"The water and mud will flood my land and damage my crops," the old man explained to Ramon when he finished the task. So once more, the tenant had to squeejee out muddy water from his house when he came home from work at night.

The old man came along as usual one morning. "Do you see that refrigerator in your house?" he asked. "Do you know how much I paid for it?"

"No," answered the tenant.

"A fortune," he said. "Close to five hundred and that was about ten years ago. Those two door ones have gone up since. I've seen them in Sears. That stove cost me three hundred dollars. I sent my son to buy it back then, around the same time. Those things are very costly, Ramon. You have to care them well."

"Well, I was planning to buy a new stove and refrigerator. The stove top is burnt off and the refrigerator leaks and stays warm," complained the tenant.

"Things these days are expensive. That is why you have to take good care. I have mine about twenty years and it's still almost brand new!" This could have been a white lie to discourage his renter from throwing away the junk.

52

The old man's attitude could be summarized in the lines of the old poem:

> 'I am monarch of all I survey.
>
> My right there is none to dispute.
>
> From the center all around
>
> I am lord of the fowl and the brute.'

He and his son went to church every Sunday, dressed in long sleeved shirts, felt hats, and pressed knit pants to pray to God for blessings and to go to heaven after death.

That night, a flashlight played on the avocado tree. The son was checking to make sure all the fruits were there.

The old man had many springs on his land, that were piped into taps in his house. So the tenant asked if he too could get spring water in his tap.

"The pump that goes to your house is broken. Actually, it worked before you came. It seems that you must have done something to damage it. If you buy a new one and install it, maybe you can get spring water in your pipe," was the shrewd reply.

If a hurricane passed the tenant would receive some green bananas, that were blown down by the wind. But the only contact he was allowed with avocados was visual --- from a distance.

It reached to a point, that he could no more bear the temptation caused by the luscious glistening fruits, so he went one night and stole two.

Next day, the old man came by blue with anger. "They should never steal from an old man like me. Ramon, did you hear any noise last night? Two more avocados are gone!"

"I did hear the neighbor's dogs barking around two this morning. It went on for about ten minutes at the most. I thought they might be seeing ghosts, so I didn't worry too much."

The old man was blowing hot and cold. "Don't worry," he said. "I'm sending my son to make a report to police that there are bandits in this area and they are stealing my crops. I worked very hard for what I have today, and whoever robs an old man like me will have to pay."

He went back, grumbling to himself, and the tenant grinned revengefully.

The old man grew cilantro for selling wholesale to supermarkets but would not give a blade to the tenant, or even sell him a dollar's worth. The tenant had to purchase it in the grocery at five blades for a dollar. So in every direction, the old man squeezed him tight.

"Ramon," he complained. "Food and medicine has gone up so high. I can't see how poor people like us could survive."

"Me neither," answered the tenant.

"What is the world coming to? I used to spend ten dollars for a doctor's visit way back then, now the fee is fifty. There is no one to protect us from these hooligans, that are ripping the shirt off our backs. All I can say is that this place needs a revolution. People must come to their senses before everything go to the dogs." He went on like a hot air merchant.

"Yes," the tenant supported consolingly.

"I believe in God and he will do for us, because this government don't give a damn!"

The old man was sturdy as his weeds and similarly set in his attitude.

One day, his wife passed away and he began to grieve quietly. He became lonely and little by little he became weaker and weaker. The inevitable diseases that attack a person his age assembled against him with trained guns. He suffered with heart, cholesterol, stroke, diabetes and a host of attending ailments. He lasted for ten years after his wife departed, until he finally succumbed and went to meet her wherever she was.

Tout le monde came to say farewell to the patriarch. His children and grandchildren wept. It was so crowded that there was no room for the tenant to get a glimpse of the funeral which was kept at home. The sons eulogized his greatness. The pastor commended his soul to heaven. Finally, he was buried on a plot of his land which he had marked out before.

The youngest son, who lived with him and had nursed him at the end, inherited his estate. His wife was not happy with the country life and nagged him constantly to sell everything and go off to New York to live. The land was laden with all sorts of crops and there were a few houses that pulled in good revenue from rent. The son himself was bored of country life — agriculture was not really his calling. He could easily get a job as handyman at any company that provided household maintenance services.

The itch to migrate was so great and fueled by the wife's

insistence, the entire property was sold off very cheap, because it was hard to get buyers. Most people were moving to the city to escape the stagnancy of country life. Ramon was able to buy his house even with the small savings he had.

The couple went their jolly way and bought a small apartment in New York where they bought avocados for five dollars each. They eventually divorced, as city pressure often makes people do. Even that small apartment was sold and the money divided. And the old man lay six feet below keeping an eye on the estate and the precious avocados that once belonged to him.

A Real Muslim

What was a Muslim cleric doing at night-time on busy street corners? Well, it was clear that he was chatting up the girls for one thing. Converting them to Allah's way? Maybe. But he was a sight and drew curious observers to wonder what in the world he was up to. And those who checked him out were not displeased or disappointed. They were amused to say the least.

He wore a long, gray beard and a Muslim hat. His clothes were not very holy. Mystic yogi pants topped by a colorful tropical shirt was his style.

He was the most popular man about town, or at least he carried himself so. There was not a more sociable guy than him. The only hitch was that no female was safe from him. His infirmity, you see, was an obsession for them, and he did everything possible to gain their favor.

He was a smooth talker, expert in moon-shining people, especially if a person had a female appearance, and one of his best means was flattery. Of course he was not a cleric. Maybe he would have liked to be one, but he used whatever knowledge he had about the religion, which was practically none at all, to try to impress others. On this island, which was very far away from the Middle East, people knew even less about Islam than him.

One night he was on his usual night rounds. A young female tourist was walking by looking confused, when he jumped to her help. "Are you looking for somewhere special, my dear? If you need any help, just let me know. A lovely young lady like you should not be out alone at night. If you need a guide, I would be glad to be one. No charge of course."

"Well thanks for your help," she said, and he went along guiding her.

A friend of his used to come into the city at night to hang out and watch ships. The Muslim made it a habit of getting into religious debates with him, although he knew not the difference between A and a bull-foot about religion. But he would crinkle his forehead, fold his arms and nod, looking up and down or staring at the sky as if in deep thought.

"Brother. I am a hajji you know. I has been to Mecca." (Of course, this was in a dream.)

"So," asked his friend. "What does this new life of Hajj mean to you?"

"Well, I feel very very peaceful and close to Allah," he said as peacefully as possible. Saying the word Allah made him 'sound' like a serious Muslim. "In fact, I would like to go to Iran and become a fakir."

"Really? You mean one of these mystics who stare?" asked his friend. "I guess fakirs meditate on Allah's name. What else could it be since Allah does not have a form?"

"You know brother, you are right. You are very brilliant. I never thought about that. Thanks for enlightening me, man.

You know brother, what you just said there is so profound. Very very profound," he said, shaking his head in deep thought. In this way he encouraged the brother to talk some more and prolong the talks, since he knew absolutely nothing. He pretended to be a deep thinker.

"I wish I could be with you all day hearing this high philosophy," he praised.

One day he brought some nuts and dates to share with his friend. "I only buy the best. Pure almonds, cashews, *mejdhool* dates, milk. It's all I eat." Someone had told him that the prophet Mohammad lived on nuts and dates. "I don't eat Planters, brother. I just can't digest it." Just then a girl acquaintance stopped to say hello to his friend. Planters, cashews and *mejdhool* dates were forgotten.

"You have nice toes young lady. Very special toes. Has anyone told you so? And I like your shoes as well. Where did you get them?" he asked.

"Well my toes are too short and I got my shoes in Payless. I paid seven dollars for them," she said.

"But I am sure everyone admires them," he said.

"I was thinking to start a business selling incense and oils on the street," he told his friend one day. "All good Muslims must sell incense and oils. I have a Libyan friend who lives in the States and who will order it for me." No doubt the Libyan friend would be buying it from someone in the States, but he was not aware of this possibility.

"By the way," he went on, "did you know that a good Muslim is allowed to have many wives?"

"I heard about this," answered the friend.

"Mr. Mustapha!" hailed a little girl who got to know him while taking evening walks with her mother.

"It's Hajji Mustapha bin Akbar, my child. Remember my dear, it's *hajji* for one who went to Mecca."

"Brother," he asked his friend one day, "can you lend me your book on the Vedas? I want to compare it with the teachings of the prophet."

No sooner had the book been lent it was ferried to a lady whom Mustapha was trying to bait with his profile of deep spirituality. He himself did not read a word of the good book. The woman's husband happened to be away on a trip, and so it was prime time to throw a bait line.

So in this way Mustapha went about his razzle-dazzle. A man who knew not a word of the Koran, never said a *namaz*, never went to a mosque or fasted for Ramadan. All he had was his beard and a few Muslim words to rally for him. But even with all his funny business he had a way of making you like him, and it worked with everyone.

"Brother, I like your Birkenstocks. It's good for Allah's work, you know. Please bring me the catalog next time you come. You said they cost ninety dollars? Okay, I will order one as soon as you bring the catalog."

But months after the magazine was placed in his hand, he still wore the five dollar plastic sandals from Kmart. So like this, he continued with his live jive pretensions day in day out.

"Mustapha, what time did you do *namaz* this evening?" asked his friend one night.

"Oh, I'll do it when I go home," he replied. That would have meant about two a. m. (and anyone could imagine that that was an impossible hour for prayers. It was then twelve midnight.)

He had a job as a mason and his friend tried to convince him that a holy man like him should have an easier job, maybe working with Kmart.

"I am very, very strict with my religion, brother. I won't cut my beard for anything. It represents wisdom, you know. You see, I was getting a job with Kmart and they wanted me to cut my beard, but I would never do that, brother. Allah would never never be pleased. I prefer to be without a job, but I won't cut my beard," he said, as he eyed some young girls going up the street and marked them out to make his move when they passed back.

This was Mustapha bin Akbar, future *fakir*, who wandered the streets at night hoping to add numbers to his list of ladies.

"Oh prophet Mustapha, I am so glad to see you." It was a fat girl whose mother had just died and whom Mustapha had been consoling a few evenings before. Now this girl was so fat---she probably weighed two hundred and fifty pounds. She wore white stretch pants despite the fact that she had clumps on her buttocks. The tight pants emphasized the clumps even more. She smelled of nice oil.

"Oh, I bought the oil you told me about from your Muslim brother who sells up the street," she said. She pointed backwards and the waves of fat on her half-bare back glowed like breasts.

"Thanks for supporting the cause. May Allah be pleased

with you." And Mustapha made plans to win her, obsessed by those clumpy buttocks. After all, he was a sixty-five year old man who did not haul in a catch too often anymore.

"She likes me," he told his friend a few days after. "I help her out. It's Allah's way. She's lonely and has physical needs, and I won't disappoint her."

And in this way the amazing future *fakir*, using the stamp of Allah's name to justify his actions, seduced yet another lady and enjoyed with her. He had already explained to his friend that a good Muslim is allowed to have many wives. And he made sure and upheld this law whenever opportunity knocked.

OM
BUDDHI
PADME
HAM !
SEE
NO
EVIL
HEAR
NO
EVIL

A Stir at the Shrine

A sanctified monastery was the setting for this unbelievable tale. A young New York immigrant and his wife were new students of meditation. This young fellow was a victim of strong lust. The pair lived in an apartment some distance from the temple. The fellow wanted to curb his heat by learning the art of self-control from the priests. He had a job and was not a full time devotee like his robed friends. His progress was slow, but nonetheless he hung in with them hoping to someday achieve their passion-less way of life.

The fellow had a few girlfriends outside marriage. These girls were living back in Trinidad which is where the couple had migrated from. On the pretext of traveling for business he would meet with them. His wife was a trusting person who had complete faith in the words of her husband. So, whenever he had to go away for two or three weeks, she waited at home and worried for him like all good wives. She was a housewife, so there was more time to miss him. The house felt lonely when he wasn't home.

The idea dawned on him to make a movie flick of one of his romantic escapades. Down to the island he went and told his favorite girlfriend about it. She agreed. They filmed the kama-sutra movie together. Raw footage of every act was recorded as the camcorder filmed the action in automatic. The hot-blooded couple exceeded themselves in the various acts and positions: inverted, normal, tangents and jobs that are too indecent to mention here.

The hour-long session was satisfactorily shot and the lovers eventually parted. The young man headed for the countryside to visit other concubines. After a week he flew back home with his blue movie to enjoy whenever the wife was out.

Not too long after that there was a big celebration in Dharmasala India, headquarters of the religion. It was the birthday of the leader who was regarded as a representative of god. Members from all parts of the world were going and the fellow decided to go, too. He made the trip together with his wife. The experience was spiritually lavish --- nothing short of divine.

The leader gave a long talk. He was covered with beautiful garlands of marigolds, jasmines and other local flowers. Incense and other articles of worship were waved at him. It was a very attractive sight. The ceremony lasted all day long. It was a get-together of nationalities never before seen, for the religion was internationally popular.

Vegetarian food was abundant and the attendees enjoyed the cool climate and enchanting scenery of that part of the Himalayas. Needless to say the fellow had carried along his video cam and never failed to shoot every noteworthy detail of the bash, as is the norm for any tourist attending such a portentous event.

The head monk was speaking about morality, the wisdom

of Buddha and other topics like reincarnation, nirvana and the peace formula for a better world. The student diligently captured every word of the address given by the guru. It was an ethereal experience and he and his wife promised themselves that this was their last life in earthly existence. They would from now on practice meditation with the aim of achieving nirvana. They planned to do one hour of mantras and meditations every morning together with lots of incense burning.

The week-long festival ended and they sadly packed their bags with as much Indian souvenirs, clothes and tapestries as could be fitted. Beautiful things. Flying back home from India, they made plans to visit every year for the occasion. The wife even shed tears. They promised each other that eventually they would move to Dharmasala to be close to the sacred master.

So back home they went to their local temple and there joined the monks for meditation as often as they possibly could.

Within a few weeks there would be another important festival --- the birthday of an important deity. The priests at the local temple would be observing it with full pomp. Meanwhile, the student viewed the film he made in India and edited it to his satisfaction. The idea was that he should hold a showing of it at the temple to mark the upcoming occasion. He was the only visitor from New York to Dharmasala that year, so he wanted to take the opportunity to share his experience with the celibates and guests who would assemble that day.

The blessed day arrived and the student and his wife fasted all day and prayed to the god for health, happiness and peace. At the temple, ceremonies were in full swing, and the chief priest had previously announced to the crowd that a film of the guru's birthday was to be shown in the evening. That brought in extra guests. In the evening time the young man reached the temple. Hundreds of people were chanting mantras. The air was thick with sweet incense smoke. He brought offerings of food for the holy men. The couple even sprinkled perfumed water on them ceremoniously.

The dove-like men accepted the gifts. The atmosphere was very pure and reverent with sounds of transcendental chants, sacred lamps burning, and the smell of holy incense. It prepared everyone's minds to receive the image of the venerated master on the large TV screen that was fixed in the center of the hall in front of the altar.

Everyone sat on mats on the ground as is the custom in oriental temples. The celibates sat in a special front row while the public guests sat in rows behind. The student was very excited to be a part of this enlightening event. It gave him bliss to serve refreshments to everyone present. So he made himself busy in the kitchen preparing trays filled with cups of tsampa --- buttered tea. The name of the revered master was chanted to invoke his presence.

The young man put the DVD in the player and went about his service in the kitchen while his wife sat in the audience to soak in the film of their great teacher and to hear the auspicious message. Every one put their palms together and bowed low on the floor. Some chanted "Om," holding their breaths for almost three minutes.

The master's sitting place came into view. All eyes were fixed on the screen as viewers lifted their heads to see the sacred show. The seat was shaking somewhat. How happy he was — always laughing just like the Buddha. They waited for his image to appear. His name was chanted once more followed by three minutes of "Ooommm."

His lotus feet now appeared and they bowed low on the floor once more. His seat shook some more as he began his lecture by laughing. His Divine Holiness was a joyful soul who was usually in the mood of the jovial Buddha. Eyes widened preparing to witness the blessed form which would soon fill the screen.

Even the camera seemed to tremble with all the happy vibrations. Some of the guests sang the famous song "Don't worry be happy" and laughed aloud.

Soon viewers started squinting their eyes and cocking their necks in different angles to try to see what was going on. The master's legs came into full view. Maybe he was tired from all the activity, so he appeared to be lying back a bit. Necks were now slanted to ninety degrees, eyelids squinted to Chinese size to get the best view — amateur filmmakers sometimes manage to film things upside down, some of them reasoned.

But wait, there was another pair of legs along with the master's. A four-legged master? No, it was a young man and a woman.. In their birthday suits? The seat was ... no it was a bed rocking from side to side.

Wait a minute! Holy shit! A couple engaged in carnal relations? Hot *kama-sutra* business! Both shamelessly nude!? Enjoying gross bodily pleasures without control! All this in the monk's temple?

Eyes widened in horror. Everyone was frozen with shock and shame. The head of the temple capsized. His shaved head

70

hit the floor. Boops!

"Good god! Save us God!" were the cries of the monks, as chaos descended into the temple. Some of the panicking ones threw down themselves in grief. Some of them covered their eyes with their palms to blind themselves. Some shouted mantras to purify their minds from the great contamination. Some rolled in shock. Some bawled and lamented. There was a grand state of confusion that evening.

The young man busy in the kitchen heard the alarm and was glad to know that his documentary was causing such spiritual ecstasy. So he called loudly from the kitchen to encourage the ecstasy: "Wait until you see the rest!"

None of the monks dared to open their eyes to witness the unholiness or even to approach the TV to turn it off. Finally, the wife managed to put her finger on the off button and the monks' agony cooled down.

The man came out to provide extra details of the birthday event. "It was a once in a lifetime experience. It was like being in heaven. Wasn't it dear? Why did you turn it off so quickly? It had just started," he asked his wife.

The pandemonium in the room was not normal though, he thought. These peaceful men never act like this. Maybe the master's presence put them in a special state of ecstasy. He grabbed the DVD from his wife's hand (she had pulled it out of the machine) to keep feeding them the spiritual treat when his eyes fell on the small hand written letters: pvte, which in his language meant "private." It was his turn to freeze with shock as he collapsed — braps! — and crashed into some cups of *tsampa* which were on the floor.

By an erroneous sleight of hand he had brought the blue

movie instead, and now every one was blue with shame. But he was the bluest of all. He quickly rose up. His breath was short and his voice stammered as if it was about to leave him.

"Dear, I tho-thought your cou-cousin had re-returned the mo-movie that he rented at the po-porn shop."

"I thought so too. I had no idea it was at home all this time," she came to his rescue, even though it was clear to every one that the man in the movie was the one currently standing before them. But the chaste wife preferred to act blind. She built up the story further: "What shame he caused us today. Dear, I always told you not to invite him home. I knew he is a very lusty person."

So the student spent half an hour begging pardon from the revered monks who were further astonished by his ability to lie. He denied and swore on the holy book that although the man looked like him, he would never dream of cheating on his wife. Why would I keep a tape at home knowing that my wife could find it?" he asked them.

"Don't worry my dear," said the supportive wife. "God knows you are telling the truth. No sin will come to you. But we must beg forgiveness from their holinesses for ruining this evening." The monks were besides themselves with disbelief at the wife's blindness. But, in order to help protect the relationship, they pretended to accept the alibi and forgave them.

The pardon was not publicly announced. The DVD was broken to bits and burned. The guests had something to gossip about for a long time. Mantras and hymns were sung all night to exorcise the demon of fleshiness that had disturbed the place. The couple was counseled to do mantras at home. And the wife and husband left with some measure of peace after repenting for causing the *melee*.

The moral of this immoral story is that a blue movie made for private viewing must be strictly guarded so that serious embarrassment of this kind never befalls anyone. End of story.

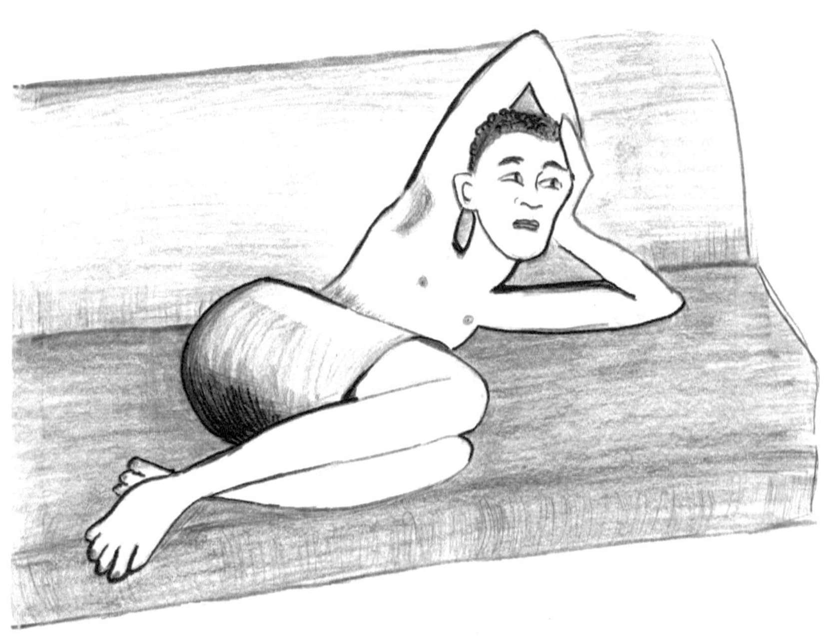

Nothingham Kulpritt

Nothingham Kulpritt lived with his wife in a government subsidized apartment. They paid twenty five dollars a month while the government paid four hundred and seventy five.

Nothingham was good for nothing and his wife blamed him for everything that went wrong. He liked nothing better to do all day than to dip his feet in a foot bath and follow everything that popped up on TV. His wife went out scraping up money for the rent and living expenses, sometimes even resorting to collecting and selling bottles.

"Nothingham could you please cook dinner? I'm going out to collect and I'll be hungry when I get back," she said one day.

No doubt he put up the beans to boil and laid back on the couch in front of the TV with his cat sleeping at his feet. But eventually he too fell asleep, and therefore when his wife returned, the beans were black charcoal stuck to the bottom of the pot. The gas tank was empty and Nothingham lay dreaming on the couch.

"Hello. I'm back; what about the dinner I asked for?" His wife jolted him awake.

"Oh, I'll check on it. Let's see ... the beans are boiling. Ow!

It burned a bit. Did you turn it off dear? Don't worry. I'll put on some more now."

"The gas finished while you were in slumber-land, Nothinghead, and there is no one else here but you to blame. Either you do the housework or go out and make some money, but you must do something," she insisted.

"Okay, tomorrow I will go out and you can rest dear. I'll go to the neighbor and see if he will let me use his stove. I can't bear to see you hungry, dear."

So off he went, but which neighbor would allow someone to boil beans on his stove? That kind of thing usually takes two hours and uses a lot of gas. Somehow he managed to convince the man that his wife was starving and very weak, and he was allowed the favor. And while the beans were boiling Nothingham sat on the neighbor's couch and glued his eyes to the TV.

Finally he came home with the meal. It was late at night, and his wife felt sorry that he was trying so hard to please her. So, she forgave him for his foolishness.

One day his wife sent him off on an errand. He was to pay the electric bill for which she had raked up some money. At nine a.m. he began to get ready for the trip. He placed the ironing board before the TV, which was on, and ironed his shirt and jeans with his eyes looking at TV unwinking.

Then he went to look for a pair of socks. "Patsy, where is my green pair of socks that matches with this shirt?"

"I don't know."

"Could you help me look for it?"

So Patsy looked drawer after drawer. She also looked in the dirty laundry basket, but they did not show up. By now it was almost ten.

"Why don't you wear another pair?" she asked.

"No dear, I must go out matching. Do you want me to look like a weirdo?"

Patsy looked and looked until a stink smell caused her to look underneath the couch, and there were the green socks, rotting where he had thrown them.

"Ah well. I'll have to use another pair," he said.

No sooner had he put on his clothes and shoes and combed his hair, he realized he had to use the bathroom. So he took everything off and went to answer nature's call.

It was almost eleven by now, and he finally finished his toilet duties and emerged apparently ready to hit the road. Then he remembered that he had to give milk to the cat, so he looked in the fridge and saw regular milk.

"Is there any non-fat milk?" he asked.

"No, I used the last bit for coffee this morning," Patsy answered. "Why can't the cat drink regular milk?"

"Because I don't want her to gain weight. I'll have to go to the grocery to get some. I'll be right back dear."

So off he went. He returned with a carton of milk and warmed it up so that the cat would not catch a cold. Then he washed the cat's bowl and filled it up. At last he appeared ready to go when suddenly a knock was heard on the door. He ran out.

"Oh pastor, please come in. I am not in a rush at all. I do have a little time to chat," he said.

Pastor entered. They both sat on the couch and engaged in small talk about church. Patsy was in the bathroom and she heard the voices.

"Nothingham, it's already twelve. Why haven't you gone out as yet?" she asked.

"The reverend is here, dear. He stepped in for a visit and I am entertaining him. You can't turn away a man of god, you know, dear. Do we have juice to give him?"

"Just look in the fridge and you will find out," answered Patsy, who was worried that Nothingham would not make it before the office closed. It just happened to be the deadline date for payment. Already the two weeks of grace period had passed.

The pastor left shortly and Nothingham went to his car and turned on the engine.

"Patsy, the battery is dead. I need someone to jump start me."

"Get the pastor to do it. I can't," shouted Patsy.

Instead of phoning, Nothingham headed to the pastor's apartment. The good man, who lived nearby, was getting ready for his afternoon siesta. Nothing entered for a while to rest his feet from all that standing and walking and told him the problem. The pastor brought over his car and proceeded to jump start the stalled vehicle. It was almost two p.m. by then and the electricity office was only open until two-thirty.

Nothingham was on the verge of leaving, it seemed, when he realized that he should pack a sandwich in case he got hungry while waiting in that long line. So, he hurried back inside, because the office would be closing soon, and packed the sandwich in foil paper so that it would not soil the car seat. He put it in a brown lunch bag. Now he was ready to go.

Half an hour left, so he pressed the gas pedal all the way. A few miles before the office, he got stuck in a nasty traffic jam. So, by the time he made it to the parking and walked toward the entrance he saw the sign CLOSED hung on the door.

Homeward he went to Patsy with one hundred and one excuses, but she could find no one to blame for the tragedy but him.

The electricity got cut off, and they remained without lights for a couple of days until Patsy found the time to go and pay the bill herself.

Urea Heaps was another friend who lived nearby in a subsidized apartment as well. He was a squat fellow who took up a lot of people's time chatting. His frequently visited Nothingham.

"Nothing," Heaps was saying one day, "you know I think we should try to make some serious money so that my wife will stop clouting me."

"And what do you have in mind?"

"Pyramid sales, of course. Get three people under you to join up and each one get three more to join up under them, and so on. Every time someone joins you get a commission."

"Yes, Heaps, it sounds like the right job for me too."

"Certainly. All you have to do is get three people, and then you can relax and watch TV all day while the money keeps coming"

The telephone rang. It was Heap's wife wondering why he was not home washing dishes and doing the chores instead of wasting time dreaming about this pyramid illusions. So, the talks ended. They both agreed that they did not have the money to invest anyway, although they had just spent about two hours planning to milk this pyramid gold mine.

Patsy was becoming so fed up with Kulpritt's uselessness that even if he did nothing she found some fault with how he was doing it. He always bore the blame for any difficulty that came up.

Another neighbor, Pastor Cuffie (They called themselves pastors. What they were doing hanging around all day, God alone knew.) was a more godly man in Patsy's eyes. So she asked him to counsel Kulpritt. He came by and from the moment he sat down he began requesting coffee. Little did she know that he had only taken the job of pastor to get handouts. Coffee was his favorite drink and he had run out of it at home.

Cuffie got his coffee and then began to talk to Kulpritt about responsibility.

"Well, I think I am a very responsible person," Kulpritt answered.

"Show me some examples," Cuffie said. "Patsy wants me to try to some instill some manly qualities in you."

"I am responsible for our poverty, or so Patsy says, and I was responsible for having our lights cut off."

"What I mean is responsible for positive things."

"I knew you were going to say that. You see my legs seem to want massaging all the time. Then I lie on the couch. And then I need to know what's going on, so I turn on the TV."

"For that, you only need a newspaper. You don't get news in movies"

"I'll try very hard to follow your advice," said Kulpritt.

"Do you have more coffee?" asked Cuffie.

"I'll make some," said Kulpritt.

Cuffie finished his counseling and went on his way.

"Nothingham," Patsy called, "do you know that the toilet is leaking?"

"No dear, thanks for letting me know," he answered.

"I don't want thanks. What I want is that you should get some tools and try to tighten up whatever is loose."

So he came in with the tool box, fumbled with the toilet, and finally managed to make it leak more. Patsy became furious and chastised him for making things worst.

"Whose fault it is now? Everything you touch breaks down. Now tell me who is responsible for this mess?"

"Lee Kin."

"What did you say?"

"Lee Kin, the owner of the building. The little bald-headed Chinese guy you saw walking around yesterday," he answered.

"The leaking problem is your fault. Before it was just a little drip. Now what am I to do?" Patsy was distraught and blamed her bad planets for ever meeting Nothingham Kulpritt.

Meanwhile, he sank into the couch before the TV as if Lee Kin would appear like a genie and fix the toilet.

Patsy, so fed up with his attitude, decided it was time to give him his walking papers. Therefore, the moment came when she finally said: "Today you have to leave this house. I can't bear your slack attitude no more. You are destroying me, and I won't have no more of it."

"Could I take the TV with me?" he asked, thinking that with the TV and car he would be able to make a start somewhere. He could go over to Heaps and ask him if he could spend the first night. She agreed for him to take the things he wanted.

So he packed up his belongings and headed for the door. Patsy was busy cleaning the apartment. He took out his things and was about to close the door behind him, as depressed as anyone could be. Suddenly he heard a crash followed by screams.

THUD! "Owh! Oh god! Nothingham!"

He looked back and saw that Patsy had slipped on the floor, which was greasy with Lestoil, and was lying there in great pain. He ran back and picked up the howling woman, who was suffering from hip problems.

"Ouch, my hip! I think it has gone out of place. I can't move. Oh, my god! What will I do? Please help me fast."

The kind but lazy Kulpritt got ready to follow instructions as to what should be done. She needed to get ready to go to the hospital. First, he had to drag his things back inside. Then, he got some of her going-out clothes and helped her get into them. Then, he got an ice bag for the hip and gave her extra strength Tylenol to ease the pain. She felt sorry for ever putting him out as he carried her to the car.

"Oh, Nothingham, what will I be without you?"

"Nothing, "he said.

"Well, nothing minus nothing makes nothing, and that is what we will be without each other. I'm sorry for giving you the pink slip," she said.

"And I'm also sorry that you slipped," he answered.

So Mr. and Mrs. Kulpritt lived happily after that time without fighting much. Kulpritt did his best to help out his wife from that time on. He looked for serious work and took a rest from the TV.

And now you know ... the rest of the story.

The Grandam of Bunkum

The Grandam of Bunkum

A dowdy dowager in her late sixties arrived in the USA from Britain. She came with money to burn because her husband had just passed away and left her a sizable inheritance. The grandam had spent all her life conservatively so she felt like loosening up. The boredom and loneliness was eating away at her and she hung out at tea shops, talking bunkum all day long to anyone who had time to listen.

Even after she had spilled out the wearisome bilge time and time again, ninnies and dopes, who had nothing better to do than sip tea non-stop and whose antennas were tired of picking up her broadcasts, continued to act as if her gossips were brand new.

A widow friend of hers tried convincing her about plastic surgery. The friend was sure that if the grandam regained her youthful looks she would even be able to attract dates and she would not be so lonely. The more the friend talked the more dissatisfied the grandam grew with her appearance until one day she buckled under pressure and started making appointments with plastic surgeons.

Although plastic surgeons in the area advertised total restoration, because of the amount of engineering needed to be done on her doctors turned her down like a cold potato. Finally, she settled a contract with one who promised to restore her to youth and give her the taut immaculate skin and looks of a twenty-two year old.

The grandam did not mind shelling out cash at the speed of a money checking machine to recover her beauty. First she would have laser surgery on her face and arms to remove freckles, wrinkles and sunburn.

The tricky doctor agreed to do the procedures on one condition - the grandam should not go in the sunlight or look in a mirror for six months. He cautioned that the sunlight or glass reflection could trigger a cancerous reaction on the raw healing skin.

She wished for a breast lift and a bottom lift, and the medico had to rent a mini forklift to lift her fallen components for they had almost dropped to ground level. Then he proceeded to implant soya gel pillowetes to increase the size of her breasts and butt and advised her to take Grobust pills to further fluff out her breasts.

Vanity is a bad thing, especially as one grows older. But the grandam was bent upon getting a boyfriend. Her friend who was also a bunkum expert convinced her that she would be able to get a boyfriend forty years younger if she only had plastic surgery.

The doctor asked the grandam what size of inserts she wanted and she replied that she preferred the deluxe size, of course. So anesthesia was given, and she came out of the operating chambers with two gel filled boobs and three gel filled bottoms. You see the medico's fingers had bungled from all that fiddling in her lower hemisphere, and he had mistakenly installed an extra gel pad in the midst of her rear.

The grandam could feel the presence of the spongy bridge in her tail but because it made her sit so comfortably and added inches to her spine she didn't say anything.

Her hair had been leaping off her head and it wafted around in tufts and handfuls, The surgeon plastered back the hair with Rogaine mixed with a touch of crazy glue to fill up the bald patches.

Vanity, oh vanity, sometimes it blinds us so much we don't care how ridiculous we look!

The surgeon asked the dame about her preference of hair color. He suggested gray-blue, for it happened to be a popular color among younger folks. The dame happily agreed to the gray-blue. Thus, the glued hair was blued.

Botox was injected in her lips and cheeks to plump them up and TCA peels were applied to her legs to even out the color for a sexy effect. She consulted the doctor about some spots on her back and he dug them out leaving holes that were similar to those of a sponge.

She underwent a spinal operation. Bamboo rods were inserted to support her spine which was doubling over with osteoporosis. This was helpful because it improved her posture and prevented her spine from tearing more. But a chiropractor's help, calcium and some exercise would have had a more permanent effect in improving the poor dame's back. When people want things to happen the easy way there is a risk of disappointment.

Some of her teeth were replaced with implants, and those which were yellowed with nicotine were bleached.

The grandam and her new skin remained indoors all day

long. Her feet were fixed in a lavender bath, and she chomped on Scottish shortbread, the ones that came in red and green plaid boxes, and sipped tea to pass time while the surgery healed.

Now she had to utter the bunkum in monologues for there wasn't a lard-head in sight to join the twaddle. Her mouth just could not keep from moving whether it was eating or talking. Some people need to keep lips flapping --- they do not have the peace of mind to even read a good book. Talk, talk, talk like a parrot is all they care to do.

In summertime her grandchildren came from England to spend holidays with granny. They were forced to return home un-holidayed since they could not recognize or even locate dear old granny who was busy working on becoming young again.

She stayed at home while surgery healed eating scones, plum pudding, sandwiches and butter cookies with her tea. Her stomach grew to such a humongous size that liposuction was recommend by the doctor. But he would do that after the six months of healing had passed, since she couldn't leave the house then. He gave her some pills called *Fat Off* which collected the fat from the food as it entered the stomach and threw it out it through the back porthole.

By this time the doctor's fees had climbed to one hundred thousand dollars which for her was a teeny sixty thousand pounds. You see the dame had no one else to share her fortune with except a little Terrier dog who fled from the house when he beheld the monster that was unfolding before his eyes, one that used to be a gentle dame not too long before.

Six months passed and healing time was over. The dame

was free to go in public, now that the surgeon had collected his fee. She was excited to show off her foxy sexy looks. Tadaah! Boyfriend time was here, and Miss Sexy was ready for action.

She practically threw on her clothes and ran to the tea shops anxious to make dates with guys who were young enough to be her sons. She had money too, so which struggling young fellow would not fall for the foxy aristocrat Dame Alice from England?

When one gets older, one should do a bit of wondering --- what lies ahead? Is there an afterlife? Where will I be in five or ten years when I die? Is there a God? How shall I prepare to meet him or her? Getting married at eighty or ninety years seems to make no sense when you look at things on this grand scale.

Unfortunately, dame Alice was not a philosophical woman. Looks, boyfriends and sex were the priorities on her mind at a time when her children already had their own grandkids.

Alice arrived in tea shop number one. "Helloooo. It's dame Alice again. The one from England. Anyone up for a cup of tea?" Alice had volumes of bunkum ready to spill on willing ears and her own eyes were sharper than a razor combing the place for a handsome dude.

But no one recognized the dame. "Ah well, new customers. Even though ... isn't that Liz and Wolfus, my old tea partners?" she asked herself

But Liz and Wolfus showed no sign of acknowledging her.

Well, if they think they are too good to hang with me, no loss, she thought. She hurried to tea shop number two which she used to haunt on Saturdays.

"Hellooo once more. Yoo hoo, I'm back. It's me Dame Alice. Just came back from England, you know. Went over for the birthday of my cousin Lord Moore and I have some great stories for you!" That intro would interest them thought the dame.

But no one seemed to care. In fact, they threw disgusted looks her way and turned their faces away.

Anyway there are no great looking guys here, she thought. I just remembered this place used to be always full of seniors. What am I doing here anyway? I'm rich, young and sexy looking. I think I'd fare better in a bar, she decided.

As she was leaving she was certain she saw the girlfriend who advised her to do surgery and a few more familiar faces. But everyone acted like they did not know her. In fact, some of them stared at her as if she had just escaped from a madhouse.

Well, she thought, it's off to the bar for me. No more tea. Who ever saw sexy young men and women sipping tea? It's about time I change my groove. Got to keep with the times, you know, she thought as she braced her palate for the hard taste of whiskey, brandy and beer.

She reached the pub. Buzz. Door opens. "Oh guys, I've been looking for this place for ages. I've heard you have the best rum and Bombay Sapphire ... Oooh guys, please fix me two drinks now. I want it now!" she shouted.

Immediately a security came grabbed her by the hair and chucked her out the door.

Crash!

What's wrong? she thought. No one is treating me right today. I must go home and tidy up a bit. I've had enough for today.

Back at home she stood in front of the mirror for the first time since surgery. BAM! She dropped to the floor and passed out. One hour later she revived. Another look in the mirror. BAM! She passed out again. In half hour she recovered. This time she took a longer look at the spook that confronted her.

Dear, dear, dear, she thought. But I thought the doctor said he would make me twenty-two again.

Of course, no doctor can do this. What they really do is pull your skin so tight it looks like plastic. Perhaps that is why it's called "plastic" surgery. When that skin starts to relax after some time there's no difference between you and a crumpled paper bag. In fact, a lady who has never had that kind of thing done to her always ends up looking like a lovely gentle angel at eighty years.

But the dame was unnaturally ambitious. She wanted to be a foxy sex kitten, but she was out foxed by a cunning doctor.

The mirror reflected :

Chalk white legs.

Blue Rasta hair.

Billy Bob chewers.

One portion of hanging bottom that looked like the ass of an ass. The gel from the rest had leaked out.

One drooping breast. The other one was flat like paper. The soy pillow had leaked out.

Green cheeks and lips. The botox had spilled over and discolored her face.

Grease spewing from her ass from all the *Fat off*.

The bamboo in her spine had broken and stuck out and turned her into a hunchback.

Pure white eyeballs. The blue contact lenses had lost their color.

A back that looked like a sponge.

And, and, and ...

Since dame Alice had chosen not to age gracefully, not even a pet cat or a pet dog could bear to stand near her. She was so grotesque. She now had to bear the pain of loneliness. She was cat-less and dog-less. Old friends wanted nothing to do with her. To clean up this mess would cost a fortune, but could she really trust a "plastic" surgeon to do it?

The dame was in a great fix --- in America, away from family, without friends, no husband, and on top of that she had become Dame Halloween.

Dame Alice swore: "Never more will I be dissatisfied," but it was too late.

She knew about god and the bible so she read at night for comfort, for not even a mouse dared scuttle in that house because of the new witch.

She regretted, swore, promised herself, lamented and suffered the consequences for trying to be what she wasn't. Now, no man, not to speak of a handsome dude, would look her way. But it was all too late. It was not easy to undo the harm. But the good thing was that the once grand lady of bunkum read, read and read and discovered a new peace from within.

And now you know --- the rest of the story.

The de la Bastide Hogpen

Dr. de la Bastide

"You're tuned in to the live show of Dr. de la Bastide on the air. The doctor is a famous natural physician as well as an MD who graduated from the Indiana School of Medicine. So get ready to call in with any questions about your health! The number is 1-800- 0234. His prescriptions are all natural and drug-free. He prescribes only herbs, minerals, and supplements.

"And our first caller is on the line. Let's take his call. Hello, you're on the air."

"Hello, Dr. de la Bastide. I suffer with high cholesterol. The grease causes my blood to clot and block my arteries and veins. My doctor gives me a lot of heavy drugs."

"You don't have to take drugs"

"What's your recommendation, doctor?"

"Well, the first thing you should do is a thorough colon irrigation. Purging out toxins is the first step in any treatment. The colon is the seat of disease according to my understanding."

"Okay."

"I do one the first thing every morning. Add a teaspoon of

lemon to a gallon of distilled water and do an enema. Keep it in for about thirty minutes if you can hold it that long."

"I will try it."

"The problem you are having is caused by an excess of low density lipo-protein and a shortage of high density lipo-protein. You will need to take the recommended dosage with each meal, which I think is three tablets each of calcium, chromium picolinate, coenzyme Q10, oat bran, kyolic, lecithin, vitamin B, vitamin C, vitamin E, flax seed oil, selenium, cayenne, pectin, ... "

"That sounds like it would put a strain on my pocket. I doubt I would be able to afford all that."

"Don't worry. If you call and place the order with the Vitamin Planet you'll get 20 percent off. It's a courtesy discount for all our callers tonight. But you have to use everything I just told you."

"Oh, I see. But doctor what can I do for my health that won't cost such a fortune? I also have three small children to mind you see."

"Change your diet. Eat strictly apples, bananas, carrots, beans, garlic, grapefruit. Use olive oil, celery juice, beet juice, spirulina juice, and lemons. Stay away from sprouts, cabbage, cauliflower, and pickles."

"Too fast, doctor. I'm getting lost."

"You know, I used to be a cholesterol sufferer myself, but once I started taking the supplements I've recommended for you and following the diet my problem disappeared overnight."

"Okay. I'm impressed. Any other suggestions, doctor?"

"Give up fast food, coffee, cakes, alcohol, sodas, creamers, tobacco, white bread, and refined food candies."

"But Dr. de la Backside --- Bastide, I won't have a life after that."

"I guarantee that my treatment will take care of your problem. Your doctor wants to destroy your liver with those drugs, and we are here to save you from that."

"And how long do you think it would take for me to see results, doctor?"

"It's different for everyone, you see. It all depends on the degree of your disease. But I insist that you place the order right away and start taking those supplements. The operator is waiting to take your order right here on the air. Let's go to our next caller. Hello, you are on the air with Doctor De la Bastide."

"Doctor de la Bastide, I suffer with high pressure. My readings are 200/250."

"That is high blood pressure alright!"

"Correct."

"I'm surprised that you're not calling from your coffin. I think I can assist you in controlling this problem. Keep monitoring it as you take these products, as recommended on the labels, three times a day with meals: calcium, magnesium, kyolic, l -carnitine, and l-glutamic acid, selenium, l- glutamine, co-enzyme q-10, essential fatty acids, vitamin c, lecithin, lipotropic factors, vitamin e, octacosonol, maitake, kelp, and bromelain. Then take multivitamin, zinc, potassium, vitamin

B, proteolytic enzymes, kyo greens and ..."

"Excuse me a minute, doctor. I'm reading here on my monitor that my pressure is beginning to climb to 250/300."

"Okay, we'll break for a commercial and then return for the rest of your consultation afterwards."

"Okay, we're back on the air with the last caller."

"Thank you, Dr. de la Bastide."

"Bio-cardio enzyme forte, *Heart Science*, maitake, shitake, vitamin a ... "

"Doctor, I suspect you have a sharp interest in my pocket book. That's a lot of money to spend on vitamins and supplements."

"You're wrong sir. I'm sorry if you're getting the wrong idea. The fact of the matter is I just work for the Vitamin Planet as a consultant. They are the ones sponsoring this program. I get no commission for sales."

"Is that so, doctor?"

"I swear it's the truth, sir, as God made morning."

"What else do you think I should I do, doctor?"

"The de la Backside, sorry, Bastide treatments always start with a backside, sorry, colon wash. You should take coffee enemas three times a day."

"Isn't that a bit too much, doctor?"

"Not really. You want a clean tunnel of health, don't you?"

"Yes, I do."

"Okay then. That's how the de la Backside, sorry, Bastide

treatment works. You also need to incorporate in your diet cayenne, chamomile, fennel, rosemary, valerian, and suma."

"Doctor, could you please go slower? I am taking notes."

"Go salt free. Avoid sodas, commercial toothpastes, soy sauce, *Advil*, *Nuprin*, animal products, cheese, anchovies, avocados, pickles, sour cream, wine, yogurt, alcohol, coffee, and tobacco."

"One minute, doctor. You're going too fast for me."

"Give up tyromine, tyrosine, fermented food, aged food, and pickled food. Get enough sleep. Do not take antihistamines. Avoid stress. Hello? Hello? Are you there?"

"Hello. Dr. de la Backside?"

"Yes. Who is this? Who am I talking to?"

"This is his wife. His pressure went right UP and he fell right DOWN. I believe it's your fault. I'll call you back tomorrow after I take care of him. Right now I have to rush him to the hospital."

"It's hard to help some people. But ... let's go to the next caller. You're on the air. This is Dr. de la Bastide."

"Hello Dr. de la Backside. I have a serious cardiovascular condition. I was wondering if you could advise me on it."

"Do you know if you have myocardial infection, aneurysm, angina pectoris, anglogram, arrhythmia, cardiac arrest, cardiomegaly, or cardiomyopathy? Isochemic attacks, carditis, cathterization, endocarditic ... "

"I am not sure which one I have, doctor. I just feel something like a deck of cards choking my chest all the time."

"First, we'll start with the colon wash as usual. Then we'll proceed to … "

"I hope I don't turn out like the previous caller."

"If you're in doubt then why, may I ask, did you call?"

"I'm just hoping for better luck. That's all."

"You will have good luck once you use my treatment. What you need to use is coenzyme q-10. That improves oxygenation of the heart muscles. Vitamin e: this is an antioxidant that reduces blood clots and prevents attacks. Selenium: at least 300 micrograms daily. Proteolytic enzymes: this prevents free radical damage to the arteries. Vitamin b complex lessens the risk of heart disease. Calcium and magnesium, 1500 micrograms daily, maintain proper heart rhythm. Glucosamine Plus helps repair the heart valves. Dimethyglicine improves heart oxygenation. Acetyl l-carmitine breaks down fat in the arteries helping to normalize blood flow."

"And I'm supposed to order all these things from Vitamin Planet?"

"No one is forcing you to buy from us, but at the Vitamin World you'd be spending twice as much for the exact same thing."

"Doctor, where is the store located in case I want to pick up the prescription personally?"

"I believe they only sell by mail. But you can place your order by calling this number: 1-212-6666."

"Don't worry, doctor. I'll see if I find the store. I also want to buy other things like toilet soap and tea tree toothpaste."

"I'm sure you won't find the place. They don't have a physical address. Even I order things from them by phone. Plus, it's not wise for a man in your condition to be running all over the place shopping. You should avoid stress as much as possible, you know. If you leave your address with us I'll see that all your supplements are mailed to you. Just remember BUYING OVER THE PHONE might prevent you from having heart failure. So I recommend that you order now from us. DO NOT WAIT!"

"No. I think I prefer to buy directly doctor. Thanks very much for your help doctor."

"Thanks for calling. Well, you can lead a horse to water, but you can't make it drink. I would order by mail and stay home and relax if I were him."

"Okay, it's time to go to the next caller. Hello, you're on the air with Dr. de la Bastide."

Knock! Knock!

"I said you're on the air with ... "

Off the air at the station: "No this isn't the air. This here is live, man. I am the cholesterol caller, this is the heart patient and this is the wife of the man who fell down. We've been looking for the location of this so called 'Vitamin Planet' and our leads brought us here. So we came to pick up our prescriptions. We are surprised to find this station is nothing but a big outlet for vitamins, and you are the big mouth vitamin pusher behind it!"

"But I am a trained naturalist."

"Trained naturalist, my ass! You're reading all this pig-latin health stuff from Dr. Balch's book. What are all these fast foods doing here? And you want to put people on diet? You tell people no alcohol and this place is stacked with Heineken, whiskey, rum, cigarettes, and cigars?

``Doctor, how come you can't heal yourself? Indiana School of Medicine graduate, my foot. We'll check up on that. You will go off the air at once, doctor. You don't practice what you preach at all."

Back on the air: "Please call in with your questions if you have any. We are sitting in for Dr. de la Backside at this time. He'll be unavailable for the next few minutes."

"Hello. Am I on the air?"

"Yes you are."

"Is this the de la Backside show?"

"Yes, but we've just taken him off the air while we do some research. The man is a fake and we are checking his credentials. Vitamin Planet could well be a money laundering business."

"Could you please put him on the air for a moment?"

"We will. But remember, it's possible that he is not a doctor at all. Alright, he's here now to answer your questions."

"Mr. Backside sir, can you explain why you are hosting a naturalist talk show and NOT PRACTICING ANYTHING NATURAL?"

"My job is simply to help people who have health problems, and I have none right now."

"We've been checking with the Vitamin World and comparing your prices. We've found yours to be three times more expensive. What is this trick about twenty percent discount?"

"It's possible that we are more expensive, but no health food store gives you quality like Vitamin Planet."

"Do you think I'll waste time checking out your quality? This health food business is a twenty-three billion dollar business, and you are one of the dirty scamps who jack up the prices of teeny little things to make poor people suffer more!"

"I only try to help people who want to improve their health and lifestyle."

Off the air: CLOUT! CLOUT! "You'll help them by selling your pills on the air at cost or face being charged for fraud. Besides, you don't have a license for resale or even a broadcast license. So it's time to liquidate your business doctor. Before these goods sink with you, sell or give them away free. BUT GET RID OF IT! Your reputation is now gone and no one will do business with you. So decide while we take more calls."

Back on the air: "Hello. Am I on the air?"

"Yes, you are on the air and talking to the cholesterol guy."

"What book was Mr. Backside reading from?"

"It's the book by Dr. James Balch. Backside knows nothing. He's a quack who reads things from people's books on the air, pretending he's a naturalist. He might soon be doing a nice service for the community by having a sale on the products. So stay with us on the air to hear his prices. You'll be happy to do business with him. Keep your fingers crossed."

"All are."

"Mr. Backside, are you ready to say something?"

"Yes. I am really, really sorry lying about the Vitamin

Planet and for saying that I am a doctor. I want to liquidate all my products for one dollar each starting now."

"Good thinking, sir. Vitamin Planet products must not go down the drain with you. We sympathize with you sir, but we also wish to celebrate our good luck. So callers, please call in with your orders. We will be here to ensure that Mr. Backside doesn't pull any more cheap tricks and that he sells everything at the price he promised. Alright 'doctor'?"

"Alright. Just help me get rid of this damn inventory so I could try my hand at something else."

"Careful! Careful, 'doctor'!"

Hurricane Jeanne

"Neighbor, neighbor, good morning!"

"Good morning to you! Nice to see you up so early."

It was Dean who called on Ralph that morning.

"Nice to see me, but what I have to say ain't so nice."

"Nothing new," joked Ralph, "but let's hear it."

"I came to say that tomorrow a big storm will be hitting and you will need to prepare for it."

"Really?"

"Yes. I just heard it on the hurricane station. You should get ready for it. Buy groceries, candles, wash laundry, nail up the windows," said Dean.

"But we just had a hurricane two weeks ago," complained Ralph.

"You said two weeks. Well *amigo*, this will not be a weak one, plus when you're in the hurricane season, they come very fast."

"Alright," went Ralph.

So Ralph began preparing for the storm. His wife put the dirty laundry to wash while they got ready to go shopping. Then she made the hurricane list — candles, matches, bread, milk, canned food, panels to bar the windows. The small electric plant was taken out, oiled and cranked to ensure it worked. They needed to buy gas for the car and fuel for the generator.

Out they went to shop, not knowing what awaited them. As they entered the first supermarket they saw that the lines were as long as the Thames bridge, so they tried another and another and it got worse and worse till they finally gave up, decided on one, took a shopping basket and began throwing in goods. Ralph raced ahead to secure a place in the cashing line to speed up things. Hurricane shopping is normally more massive than Christmas or Thanksgiving, and stores raise the prices of perishable goods like bread and milk, etc.

Next they rushed to buy panels to board up the windows. Pandemonium was breaking loose as store closing hour drew nearer. Shoppers drove off in pick-up trucks full of panels, galvanize, lamps, and other hurricane necessities. The next stop was the gas station. This was a strong test of the virtue of patience for there were no less than fifty vehicles waiting to buy gas. Ralph hurried to the next station.

After running around trying to find a station with less customers, he finally lined up and put in ten dollars of gas which turned out to be half the quantity he normally got for that price, since prices had naturally doubled in the last twelve hours.

Then they hastened home to board up the windows. His wife packed away the goods and he brought the panels to the window and set them down.

"Oh shucks, I forgot to buy nails. Denise, run over to Mr. Torres quickly and borrow some."

Denise raced over, out of breath. "Neighbor I need some nails for Ralph to bar the windows."

"Sure, take all you need. I bought five pounds this morning," Torres said. She ran back home with a brown paper bag full of large nails.

A while later the phone rang. It was Dean. "I heard on the news that the storm has developed into a powerful hurricane and will be hitting us tomorrow with force. Please don't forget to bring in your potted plants and pets."

"I did it already," answered Ralph. "Have you secured your horse ?"

"The horse is in my garage," Dean answered. "Well I think we're ready for her. The name is Jeanne. Remember: keep candles and matches handy."

"I will," replied Ralph. "You have batteries to listen to radio news?" he asked, as he made a mental note to remove some old batteries from a tape recorder to power his radio later on.
 "I think we're finally set. But I'm worried about my car parked in the open."

"We just have to pray that it keeps safe," said Dean.

"Well then, goodnight and good luck. Remember that Jeanne is scheduled to hit at dawn; so stay alert."

"OK. Good luck to you too neighbor," bade Dean.

108

The previous day was disturbingly humid. Not a drop of breeze stirred in the sky. Today the weather was strange as well. At two P.M. the sky darkened. All businesses had closed by that time. The only ones open were "hurricane" stores and gas stations which were spilling over in the four directions with clients.

The day had been cool and seemed normal. There were glimpses of sunlight and sometimes the sky was clouded over, but by three P.M., Jeanne has seriously announced her coming by darkening the horizon and drizzling profusely. Traffic snailed painfully, and it took ages for folks to make it to the safety of their homes. Many of them refused to wait at the stations to get gas.

Before going to bed, people played the TV to hear the latest movement of the hurricane. Candles and matches were placed next to beds, as the island waited for Jeanne to march in.

The night was still and calm. All the night insects and creatures could be heard singing as if it was the last symphony, reminding one of the orchestra which played while the Titanic sank. Even birds could be heard chirping, for the night was strangely still. There was no sign of rainfall. The temperature kept dropping. Rain finally arrived in the pre-dawn hours. Everyone, even those who slept, held their breath waiting for the action. By six A.M. the rain strengthened and fell incessantly, keeping many under their blankets although they were already awake.

Around seven A.M. Dean came around in his raincoat, sheltered with a black parasol.

"Neighbor, thank god it passed. That was a short one!"

"It ain't pass, if you want to hear the truth. It's just starting," bellowed Ralph.

" Oh god, then I have to run home and tell Maria. She was just about to wash and hang laundry."

So the neighbor sped back. Jeanne prepared to break loose. The winds started whirling around and around as she got ready to lash out. Rains pelted down and moved from place to place, house to house with force. The winds and rain rose and dropped in circles. Sometimes they roared, and then they fell into a whisper, and Jeanne got ready to unleash her might.

Ralph turned on the radio and heard that sixty people had been killed in Jamaica, thirty in Grenada. Waves had risen to a record thirty feet in Trinidad. Boats were swept up in the air and residential areas had been destroyed. Some places were under floods. This year's hurricanes seemed determined to punish all those in their path.

His wife heard the radio broadcast and remarked, "Sad to hear the bad news, but as you know we here are god-fearing people, and we usually get spared from the bad ones."

"Well if you're so god-fearing, get on your knees and pray so that the car don't get smashed today," said Ralph.

" No problem. Hail Mary. Hail Mary ... " she started.

By nine A.M., Jeanne made it known that she meant business, and in a fit of fury started seriously assaulting the island. She roared and whispered intermittently as the bending trees made their own swishing sounds. The power had long been cut off, and windows remained tightly shut. Candles burned in every room, which would otherwise be dark as night.

Ralph left a door of his house cracked open to get a view of the action. There was nothing to be seen but the color gray. All shapes and forms were totally obscured by blasts of rain and a gray-black sky.

The neighborhood boys ran around in shorts, drenched, enjoying the gushing rainfall, which thrilled their senses.

"I gotta bring in my donkey," shouted Juan.

"Yeah let's do it," said his friends.

So they untied the soaking animal and ran him off to shelter.

The winds pounded the roofs and houses. The sound was deafening. Nine A.M., ten A.M., eleven A.M., twelve A.M.. The noise of winds, rain, swaying trees, crashing, and then falling to a whisper— as the satanic sky lashed out in a fit of wrath. The sky roared, stopped, then roared again, as man and beast fearfully waited for the angry goddess to depart.

It was a day of extreme anxiety, suspense, fear, and surprise for people, and happiness for "hurricane store" owners who counted their loot and prayed for another one to come.

By one P.M., the tempest was moaning and pummeling the earth. Animals tried to enter houses. Roofs pounded. Loose galvanize and anything that was not bolted down flew away in the powerful gusts like kites in the sky. Jeanne whirled around and around battering like a battering ram. By two P.M. everyone realized that she was a supernatural, uncontrollable diva, bent on destroying those below.

At three pm she was still thundering. Unstable roofs flew away. Giant trees were uprooted. Mountains of mudslides blocked the roads.

Neither man nor beast dared to stir in the dreadful outdoors. Ralph powered his TV with the generator and looked at the hurricane station as the broadcaster kept informing, "It's a very large system. Winds are 65 miles an hour and it's crossing very slowly. By evening it will reach the northwest of the island and will increase to seventy five miles an hour. By midnight it will exit the island."

Meanwhile avocados and coconuts flew in the dark air like missiles. Tree branches sailed high in the clouds. Winds and rain crashed against houses, while people huddled inside with cups of hot tea, coffee, or other comfort drinks. Some chanted "Hail Mary Mother of God" on beads, as Jeanne ravaged the place. Rains pelted down. The heavens became furious, and all hell broke loose.

All creatures took to hiding, no one knows where, but somehow dead insects and birds are hardly ever found after a storm. By four P.M., Jeanne continued whiplashing the mountains with a mean anger. Chants of "Hail Mary" rose to a louder pitch, and a coconut broke the windshield of Ralph's car which caused even him to do a "Hail Mary," and blame himself for not praying earlier.

The sky remained fierce and showed no sign of relenting. All remained bolted indoors, and Jeanne kept bombing the place with all her fury — roaring, whistling, whipping, slapping, flooding, and frightening the hell out of people, who waited with arms folded, for her to leave.

Rains poured and lashed. Cats which were not normally allowed inside were invited to spend the day indoors. Now and then, the shouts and whistles of the neighborhood boys who were the only souls to risk their lives outside for the sake of fun, echoed whenever the wind fell into a whisper.

Jeanne kept cracking down without any mercy. "Hail Mary" didn't seem to work, as plantations of bananas, citrus, plantains, lay on the ground like colonies of slain armies. Gods seemed to pelt meteorites from the skies. The ground was strewn with leaves and branches. Rivers left their banks, and trees appeared to dance eerily as the strong gusts gave them a good flogging, their leaves shed, like hair ripped from heads. Soft flexible trees endured the beating, but those which did not bend easily snapped into two. Calabash trees prayed to their gods for help. Winds beat against boarded windows like demons knocking to enter.

Torchlights joined candles, lanterns and flambeau to provide light in homes which were pitch dark.

As the tempest began to navigate its course to the northeast of the island, the winds subsided into a whirring rush. The rain lessened its intensity, and some of the darkness began to lift off. But the gusts kept flicking against windows incessantly, like a lunatic whose mind cannot be consoled. Flower gardens were destroyed and flowers flew about in the sky decoratively.

The wind continued whirring, heaving, rising, dropping unforgivingly; Ralph and Denise stopped their "Hail Marys," and Torres, a converted Hindu, stopped his "Ram Ram" chant to go sip some black coffee.

He reasoned that although the name Ram was a name of God, it also meant force in today's language. So if he stopped uttering the word Ram the force would end.

At five P.M. the blasts whipped stronger and stronger, roaring like the wild Atlantic ocean, then dying down, up and down, up and down.

Jeanne was scheduled to leave at midnight and she kept up the pressure throughout the night, until one A.M. at least, appearing to stroke the island passionately with her tail, sprinkling water nonstop. The wind grew gentler, rustling all night, not in a frightful way, but just enough to keep people buried under their blankets.

Coquis and insects began singing their night songs from one A.M. onward, answering the cries of the dying winds.

By morning the fear factor totally disappeared, but the sky remained gray all around, threatening immense rainfall. The roads were strewn with debris, landslides, trees and leaves. Cocks resumed crowing. Power remained off and schools, many serving as shelters, were shut down.

Ralph got up next morning and at once turned on his radio to listen to the damages. Soon Dean showed up. "Well thank god it's over," he shouted. "I'm going to drive around and see how things are looking."

"Thank god we're alive," answered Ralph. "If the road is drivable, I myself will do that later on. I would also like to remove those panels as soon as possible. Man, I can't live in a place that is as dark as a cave."

"Remove what panels? You listen to the news day and

night and you don't know that another storm is coming next week? One named Lisa?"

"WHAT?"

"I said another storm is coming next week," yelled Dean.

And with that Ralph picked up an avocado and stoned Dean. "Get away from here, messenger of doom." Dean dodged the buttery missile and hopped home laughing, happy to get another chance to tease his friend.

So Ralph left the barricades on and began to brace his mind for the next week's adventure.

Puerto Rican Jackfruit

The Legend of the Puerto Rican Jackfruit

Just in front of the entrance of the main tower of the University of Puerto Rico, Rio Piedras, three paths meet. The entire complex is shaded by exotic tropical trees, but the path that leads left is lined with stately handsome jackfruit trees, a tree which had its origins in India.

These jackfruit, called *kowah* in the West Indies, are the heaviest tree-borne fruit alive — one can weigh up to forty pounds. It is melon shaped, and the outer surface is hard and prickly. The fruit grow out of the upper trunk of the tree as well as the branches. On campus they are left to mature and ripen on the trees, because no one knows their value or even that they could be eaten.

It is also little known that just as much as passersby are unaware of them, jackfruits are aware of all who pass up and down beneath them. These fruits, you see, can grow almost to human size, and apparently possess intelligence. They despised being ignored for so many years.

Fruits that grow up to two feet long, with almost five hundred pulp-covered, yummy seeds and no one notices? It was a very painful situation for them indeed.

The only information people care about was their botanical name — something freaky like 'Artocarpus

Heterophyllus' — which is etched on a label nailed to the bottom of the trees.

In places like Vietnam, these trees are given due respect; even Buddhas are carved from their trunks. Certainly it is recognized as an enlightened tree. Whether green or ripe the fruit are eaten with gusto all over Asia. But not here on this island. A little shade was the only worth placed on them.

Once, the chairman of the Council of Jackfruits called a meeting and asked all the resident fruits to submit plans which would help draw due attention to them. These jacks were slow-witted; one of them on his own could not come up with anything that made sense. The trees had been on campus for almost fifty years, and everyone was using the glossy green foliage for shade, but no notice was taken of their mammoth fruity occupants.

A plan emerged after much discussion and thought: one of them was to land on the head of a pedestrian below. Normally, when they became fully ripe, the stem would detach and they would drop to the ground and smash into bits. So it seemed to them that someone's head should serve as a shock absorber for the falling titanic jack.

The problem was selecting the suitable head. Some heads were too triangular, slicing could possibly occur, some were too round — a roll off effect — while some were egg shaped — even faster roll off. There were Afro heads — the risk of bumping off — and heads that wore large curlers, which could catch and imprison the seeds. Some of the rasta heads were too odorous. So they all sat, with their faces in their palms, and worried and prayed for the right head to come along, and one day god sent it to them.

"I hereby select that professor of Information Technology who passes every morning around ten," announced the cumbrous old chairman, whose time to drop was coming close.

"You mean the one with the square head?" asked his awkwardly bulky wife.

"Precisely. His head is big and square and I might not even roll off. It would be like landing in a sofa. He has a full soft head of hair — the right cushioning that I need."

"Good thinking," said the wife. "I wish I could be so lucky when my time comes." Every one in the council stood up and clapped, and since the grounded folks never looked up they thought it was just leaves rustling in the wind.

The professor of IT was a man who sometimes practiced the headstand yoga exercise. The reason was that he was trying to lose some weight and get his blood to circulate in both directions, for though it flowed down, it hardly flowed up to his brain. So the headstand ensured a two way flow; plus it helped straighten out a certain physical flaw that made him very conscious around the girls — he had a big belly and his legs appeared too thin to carry them. The stand killed two birds with one stone, and the professor now walked with more confidence.

Normally he felt the need to pull in his tummy when there were girls around. Now, with the help of waist tightening jockey shorts, all he had to do was inhale and the pulling in was much more effortless. Since the university population was three quarters female and one quarter male, well, he was inhaling three quarters of the times and exhaling only a quarter of the time. He always carried a laptop, to practice his IT. But sadly, though he was a genius of Information Technology, and he watched the world through the lap top, he was blind to the fact that he was being watched by some massive fruit almost as weighty as himself.

It was unfortunate that the professor did not also realize that the headstand had gradually flattened the top of his head, which was rather big to accommodate a lengthy brain coil. Smart people usually are fitted with more yardage, so their heads are more sizable. The flatness of his head gave it the appearance of a plateau covered with black grass. At least this was how the council chairman saw it from where he was sitting.

"Here he comes. What do you think?" the jackfruit chief nudged the others. And they looked down to check him out, as he walked by. One of them let out a wolf whistle, he was so hyped-up, but the folks below thought it was only the birds singing.

"Perfect," said another one. "No slopes and the acreage is ample."

So these naughty fruit made their mischievous plans. It is said that coconuts also have eyes, because no one has ever been hit by one. They are a kinder and gentler bunch.

The one chosen for the drop off job was no doubt the elderly chairman, for he was about six months old and about forty pounds hefty. "Boo-hoo, please don't leave me," cried the wife. But he had no choice in the matter. He was over ripe and his tonnage was becoming a back-breaking problem for his stem. So next morning the professor strutted along with his starched walk, back straight, and breath inhaled, the laptop, and the square head. The jackfruit gathered to cheer, "Hip Hip Hurray," and some of them sang *Auld Lang Syne*, while the old fruit aimed and readied to tug at his stem at the precise moment. There was no need to, though, for the stem just gave way on its own and "PLOPS!" Down he fell.

What a disappointment it was. He fell just behind the professor's back, and the lucky man escaped unscathed; what is more he was so much into his prim world that he did not even notice the accident.

It was a fascinating mess. The yellow pulp was as fragrant as a perfume made from bananas and pineapples, and it spread everywhere with the wind. The stem splashed a white gummy latex on the pavement. A few birds swept down to enjoy the feast, but their human counterparts went by with rigid necks, and even declared the smell was too sweet for their noses.

Eventually, the janitor was called to clean up the luscious mess, and the poor birds had to abandon their ambrosial meal. The fabulous fruit was scooped up, put in a black garbage bag and shoved in the dump, by the ignorant cleaner. The onlooking jackfruits wept, in their tree house, but none of them could do any thing about the situation, because their language was different from human's.

The wife was a few days younger than the deceased chairman, and about five pounds less weighty, and she could not stop the tears from flowing, even when the next day came. At ten sharp, the professor walked by with his plumb back and pulled-in-stomach — he was also an expert in a different kind of IT — Inhaling Technology.

In the tree top she was still shaking with grief, and she was bursting ripe and pregnant with five hundred seeds, covered with pulp, which, when roasted are similar to chestnuts. "Oh my dear husband!" she was wailing, when suddenly, her fifty five pounds broke loose from the trunk and "PLOPS!" Smack on the professor's head she landed! She did not roll down but sat there for a moment, until her whole body started to crumble. The professor thought he had been hit by a cannon ball or maybe a UFO. His breathing quickened, and inhalation and exhalation became even.

"Ooh! Oh! Oye! Ooye! Oooye! " he shrieked as the crashing fruit impacted him, and threw him on the ground. The white glue from the stem ran all over his body, and he was quickly buried under five hundred yellow, juicy seeds. The birds pounced down at once, but were shooed off by astonished onlookers. The poor man squirmed in pain and called out, "Help! Help!" There was a pile of nuts lying on his chest — chestnuts — and he became the Nutty Professor Number Two.

He did not have to cry too much for help. Quickly, about a hundred people gathered, and before before you could say "Jack Rabbit," an ambulance was called. The crowd which was frozen with shock did not clean up the mountain of seeds that covered him. They were so confused. The ambulance driver had to spend his time doing it, before loading the fragrant professor in the van. Then he sped off to the hospital, with the horn sounding full blast. In the fracas, even the laptop — center of Information Technology — got lost and the professor almost became unconscious and information-less.

The janitor was off duty at the moment, so the odoriferous mountain of yellow seeds was left for a while, filling the air with a sweet aroma. An Indian professor happened to be passing by when he noticed the delectable waste. Immediately he stooped down and started stuffing his mouth with the treat, and spitting the brown seeds out into a bag. By his prompting, many others joined the party, including birds, a rasta-artist, a hippie professor from Spain, a woman carrying a baby (for the professor had explained to her that the jackfruit created milk for nursing mothers), and many of the young students as well. Even a steely old professora sat down to the feast.

It was a day of victory for the jackfruits. They got the recognition that they deserved, and they all gave a big hand of applause at the scene. The crowd below heard them clapping, looked up and cheered back. The dean of the campus came upon the happy scene, and after listening to the Indian expounding the merits of the bulky fruit, declared that from that day on they would be duly harvested in the most fitting way. A net would be strung below the fruits like a hammock to catch them, so that they would not suffer pain and breakage from hitting the ground.

The seeds would be served in the university café, and turned into drinks and ice cream. No longer would they end up in the garbage. The giants above applauded the new decree — while the dean gorged himself on a handful of seeds.

The professor was hospitalized for a day and given a stitch on the head, for a stitch in time saves nine. He was back on his job a few weeks later, bought a new laptop and paid more attention now to his surroundings, than to inhaling. He lost some weight due to the head-on collision, and his image was reduced in the eyes of girl students, who had laughed without shame at the poor man's tragedy.

He used to eat in the cafeteria, and he noticed that everyone was patronizing this jackfruit in the form of fruit salad, sherbets, et cetera, but the professor of IT never ever partook of one seed — small revenge, but it was satisfying enough for him.

Matata Talula

Once, a dog and a half lived together. Now, do not get dumb-fumbled here, my friends. They were two. I mean there was a normal sized fluffy, and the other one was a half sized fluffy puffy thing. But whenever you lined them up together, they looked like one and a half.

They named themselves — the big one called herself Brown Sugar, and the small one went under the moniker White Sugar. This was based on the pigmentation of their coats, for they only cared about physical looks, color, and nothing else.

They were very close, and quite proud of themselves. They ate meals, drank water, and partied together. If platform shoes were in fashion, they would be seen sporting them like two models. In other words this one and a half dogs were like twins.

They grooved by themselves and thought that none was better than them. And they believed and said that most dogs of the day were low and ugly. And they were the only ones up there, with the goods — top-of-the-line productions.

Now a friendless gray dog who had no company to chill with, went to check them out, to see if they would play with her. She found their residence easily for there was a large sign outside that read: THE SUGARS.

"Good day, my friends. I is the only other dog in town, and I sometimes feels quite lonely. Today is one of those times. I cames by to see if you would plays with me and give me a good time, because I is maxed out with depression."

"Why certainly not. How dare you ask? Can't you see we are fat, high-bred top dogs and you are just a long, skinny pot hound. Having a low gray-hound like you mixing with us would be very humiliating. Please go back to your home, and don't bother us. Fast and out of place, little scoundrel!" Brown Sugar and White Sugar shooed her off and laughed, and continued to merry themselves.

"Bye then," was her humble reply. "Matata Talula."

So the lonely gray hound went home crying and woke up with a plan next morning. She dipped herself in a bucket of pink paint and went back once more to talk to the twosome.

"Me name is Pink Sugar. Can you become me friends? I just moves in the area, and I don't know no one else here."

"Don't you think we recognize you, scoundrel? You are no one else but the low gray hound who came by yesterday. You had a chip in your ear and one on your shoulder, and your eyes are still full of eye jam, like yesterday. Please, you don't fit into our league at all. So give up your tricks. Us handsome gals don't need unhandsome chicks like you around."

"I'm sorry, my friends. Matata talula," she said in her usual dejected way.

So Pink Sugar went back home, with her tail tucked between her legs, and crawled into her kennel and wept with misery and loneliness. But the luckless dog had forgotten to wash off the paint before it got dry, and next day it felt like cement plastered on her. So she had no choice but to jump in a bucket of paint remover, and after a while the paint shelled out, but she was also left with no coat, for all her fur was pulled out as well. And Brown Sugar and White Sugar pampered their soft long shag with shampoo, hair conditioner, and emollients.

The same day entered on the scene another dog who came from a faraway town called Mississippi. Now the doggess, for it was a she, was named after the said town, and she called herself Missy for short.

Everywhere she went she carried a bottle with a yellow foamy liquid, which she drank from when she was thirsty. She came upon the lonely, scraggy Pink Sugar with her bare skin, and they became friends. Pink Sugar invited her to have a bowl of water, but she declined saying that she had her own quencher. And besides, she said, she didn't drink tap water because of the chlorine content which could cause kidney stones.

Then Missy took out her bottle, had a pull with an organic straw, capped the bottle, and put it away safely, lest the precious drink became misplaced.

"I is curious to know what is that you is having. It does looks like beer to me," Pink Sugar asked.

"Oh, this is a special protein which I take every day. It destroys kidney stone. It's not like the tap water that causes stones."

"And where from you buys it?"

"I make it myself."

" I sees, very very interesting. Do you has a name for it?"

"Leek fluid."

"You means like onion juice?"

"No, my friend, urination. Urination in simple language is piss, comprende?"

"Si, senorita. Matata talula." Pink Sugar did not want to wear out the patience of her only friend.

"And it keep you healthy?"

"Of course my friend. How do you think I walked from Mississippi?"

On saying so, Missy took out the bottle and took a Lilliputian sip.

"Ah! I sees what you mean: 'Missy — sip — pee.'" Pink Sugar knocked her head for not thinking of it before. So the two kept each others' company and the days passed and Pink Sugar did not feel unwanted any more. The days were no longer dreary, and they went quickly in the company of her new lady friend.

Some time flew by. A new dog appeared on the block and introduced himself with the quaint name Chuckleberry Grin. He added a touch of gaiety to the duo's life, by doing things like hopping backwards on two legs, headstand and tail-stand yoga, the flip, and salsa dance for which he played rhythm with his mouth.

He made the two friends chuckle and grin so much, and when they got thirsty, he went in search of berries and made them berry punch. And the three of them lived like twins.

They lacked no company for theirs was the sweetest around —
the health freak Missy, the clown Chuckleberry, and the naked
backed Pink Sugar, who even forgot about the insults from
Brown and White Sugars.

Now it happened that there was a tick plague hitting the
town, and the five dogs were in great danger of extinction. The
ticks searched up and down the borough, but could find no
more than five dogs to invade. So they went to work. In a
short time Brown Sugar and White Sugar's coats were crawling
with ticks, and they buried themselves deep down in the layers,
for there was no exit through the maze of shag.

The two doubled in weight because of the mass of ticks
that was drilling into them. Brown Sugar now climbed from
forty to eighty pounds, and White Sugar from twenty to forty
pounds. And no weight-loss programs could do anything for
them.

And these ticks sucked and sucked the life out of these
poor brutes, and no one was around to assist them. After some
time, Brown Sugar borrowed a weed whacker to try to graze
the ticks out of her friend, but accidentally, she sliced into
some flesh with it, and the half dog dropped dead.

A human neighbor noticed that the bigger Sugar could
hardly walk with the heavy load of ticks, which were
consuming her like leeches. So he went to Home Depot, bought
some Tick Be Gone and sprayed down the dog, and the ticks
died. Then the kind neighbor instead of letting the dog go
around with a body full of rotten ticks, used a regular lawn
trimmer and mowed off her tickish fur.

Some of the Tick Be Gone had seeped into her skin, and she

was beginning to feel ill. Anyway, she walked around to see if she could shake off the drowsiness, till she finally reached the area where the three friends lived.

Now, they were saved from the merciless ticks. You see, Pink Sugar was coat-less since the time she submerged herself in the bucket of paint remover. The ticks therefore had no place to hide and reproduce, for they only stay in forested areas for protection reasons. Pink Sugar was well known as a streaker.

When the ticks discovered Missy and tasted her blood they spat it out in disgust because of the bitter leeky taste. So they climbed off her back and retraced their steps to get far away from the odor. Chuckleberry was saved because he was always frisking around doing yoga or some sort of silly prance. So that whenever the ticks tried to settle down on him they would be violently shaken off.

Slowly, Brown Sugar made it to where they lived, and knocked on their door. And Pink Sugar recognized her, and the yams in her eyes which were nothing but dried tears. And she felt sorry.

"Come in from the sun and sit down. You looks much smaller than the last time I sees you. Tell me what is your troubles.?"

"Well, the tick plague which you might have heard about finished off White Sugar," a technical lie since she was the one who shaved off her friend's flesh. "Since I have no one to help me in Dogswood, I figures I should walk around and do a little thinking, which is what I was doing when I stumbled into your place." This was another untruth because the wretched dog was hopeful of encountering Pink Sugar once more, to gain her help and friendship.

"Well we here is a warm and friendly bunch. Isn't we, Missy?"

"Matata Talula." Missy had picked up the slang used by people of very dark or gray color to mean that all was OK, but many times she would use it out of context. She nonetheless wanted to show off her fluency in ethnic languages.

"We always likes to do a good turns to anyone who come for helps. Right, Missy?"

"Matata Talula." Pink Sugar restrained a hearty grin, which almost busted out of her cheeks , as she tried to keep it down, and Brown Sugar was impressed by the fancy vocabulary.

The ailing dog was seated on a cushion, and Pink Sugar oiled her down with Johnson's Dog Oil, and Chuckleberry Grin spun on his head and made her laugh her head off.

"Would you like to have a drink? I am sure you must be very thirsty," asked Missy.

"Matata Talula," answered the sick Sugar. She was already getting the grip of the language and feeling right at home. Pink Sugar broke out in hysterical laughter, almost frothing at the mouth. "I surely am thirsty after walking all those miles, but I was so ashamed to ask, since you all have been so nice to me."

"No need to feel ashamed here," called Missy, who headed to the back with a heavy bladder. The warm frothy beverage was emptied into a bowl and brought out and presented to the weakened dog. She sipped it and disliked its bitter pungent taste, but due to not wanting to look ungrateful she said: "It is quite good actually. What is the name of it ?"

"It's Leek juice," Missy replied. "Like in onions."

The dog shook her head affirmatively to show that she was also knowledgeable.

"It will bring you back to health, and your shag will grow back in place, because I know there are some juices which make hair grow back in the wrong area, such as on the soles of the feet."

"Yes, I've seen those," answered Brown Sugar, pretending to know, in order to prolong the attention of the conversation. Then she gulped down the whole bowlful of the beverage and thanked Missy for being so helpful and caring.

Then the brown pooch wrote a note on a piece of a brown paper bag :

MY DeeR DiNGoS,

THaNKS FOR Taking Me iN aND SHoWiNG So mUch LOVe aND CaRE WhEN I KNeeDeD IT. I HeREbY aPPLY FoR ASSYLuM IN YoUR DoGHouSE, BeCauSE I LiKe YouR DoGMaS.

YOUrs ... DOggEDLee,

B. S.

The application was accepted. and the four lived happily ever after.

Police Madness

Superintendent Yubeedam was head of his division.
Under his command were officers like Sergeant Bozo, Sergeant
McLoud, Lieutenant Quail, Constable Piggott, Constabless
Rosasharn, and a Chinese guy called Constable Bum Fatt.

As you may be guessing, the town was a hot bed of
mischief and crime, as long as this mickey-mouse force had the
job of watching over it. A spate of kidnappings had been
hitting the area for six months. One day, the super decided to
get busy and called his men together.

"As we have been hearing and reading, there is a series of
crimes taking place on a daily basis, and the situation is
becoming very serious. I know that you boys are a ring of
jokers, but I would like to see us wake up and take action. You
sit around here all day jerking off, and my precinct is getting
the reputation that we ain't doing nothing. Our reputation
must not be spoiled. I want to see some arrests being made!"

"But Mr. Yubeedam, we have just been doing whatever you
tell us," answered Bozo.

"I want strict silence when I speak. Now just go out and
hold someone before I blow up all of you!"

Bozo, Piggott, Quail, and the rest of the gang left with

caffeinated heads looking for someone to pay the cake, while the boss and Constabless Rosasharn remained behind to clear up the coffee cups, and make private interchanges.

"Now I always tell these fools to act like they are doing something for their money, never mind what I do, but they won't hear me," he complained to himself.

An hour later the group came back with a catch all done up with handcuffs.

"I am an innocent man with family. How could you charge me for kidnapping without any proof whatsoever?" he pleaded.

"Don't worry, we will come up with the evidence," the superintendent assured the distressed prisoner.

"Bozo, Piggott, and Quail, get busy fixing up some evidence on this guy, before I give him a good beating for verbal abuse, or his lawyer gets here!" He ordered. "Bum Fatt make yourself useful. Put on coffee to brew, immediately!"

Eventually Rosasharn emerged from Yubeedam's room, where she was resting, and almost fainted.

"You have arrested my poor uncle, you idiots! What is the reason for this? Get him out of here at once!" she trembled with rage.

"Well we couldna find no one else, and it was getting close to mealtime so we just hauled him in," explained Piggott.

"Set him free if you know what is good for you before I set Yubee on all of you," she howled.

The man was freed and the quaking gang headed out once again to try their luck, before Yubeedam reentered the scene.

Just around the block they encountered a loitering student with a full grown beard and extremely dark sunshades. "He looks like a terrorist all right," thought Bozo, so the man was dragged in.

Yubeedam had heard of the previous arrest from the lady officer, so he asked with caution eyeing her: "Is this man related to anyone here?"

"No," everyone chimed.

"Okay. Cool runnings. Quail and others get working on collecting evidence," and with that he went back into his room, with a package of cigarettes and the coffee pot.

Around ten pm. the crew retired to take rest for the night, when the radio signal started to buzz. Emergency! It was Constable Piggott who had gone out for night breeze — he wanted to know if anyone was interested in fast food — what would they like. Everyone placed their orders; even Quail, who was not related to the famous politician named Dan, woke up for a share of the midnight feast.

Bum Fatt was a local recruit who was hired just to increase the numbers, and he was being trained by his seniors in police matters. So he was taken outside for solo marching instructions, under the directions of McLoud.

"Left, right, left, right," went McLoud.

" I mean march! Not wagging your fat bum from left to right," he continued to scream.

"But we are in June, sir, it's not March as yet."

"Like this," and he showed the constable how to do it.

"Left, right, left, right," Bum Fatt imitated, and raced back inside to put up coffee for the super.

"I'll wring your neck," McLoud screeched, though he was quite glad that the session was so short.

That night he took an urgent telephone call — there was an armed robbery two blocks away, and police assistance was requested.

"Tomorrow after breakfast we will send someone over. Go to sleep and try to rest it off for now," he shouted over the phone. The tired crew went to rest early that night.

"Let it be known," Yubeedam said one day, "that no citizen shall carry mace or pepper spray, once I am in charge of this precinct. If these things go off, innocent people will be injured. It will always be outlawed once I am in charge. Those who are qualified to use these items will have to fill up the necessary applications and apply for a license. A permit may be granted in a year's time if I approve of the application."

McLoud, as usual, was delegated to issue the press release.

And innocent people who were denied mace and pepper spray were kidnapped, raped, and robbed, while Yubeedam upheld strict laws prohibiting their use. The head of this amazing court of errors issued another decree:

"Let it be known that possession of arms of any sort, including firearms is illegal. Innocent persons could be harmed. No one in this town, including you officers should be armed. Any queries on this matter should be forwarded to me."

He sat back and waited to be applauded by the media, but was disappointed after a very short while. The only guntoters in town then were the criminals, for Yubeedam had deemed it so.

The officers planned a party for Rosasharn's birthday, and the police station was swinging that night. Music blasted accompanied by eating, drinking and merrymaking. A neighbor appeared to lodge a complaint because he could not sleep. McLoud tried to bribe him.

"Please come in and have some cake." He did, and that calmed him down for the time being. Next day the papers printed that the public was extremely fed up with Yubeedam and his screwy sidekicks.

There were ongoing murders, robberies and rapes, but the police battalion was on full time holiday, so it seemed. Kidnapping was rampant, while the super and his men played it cool. One day he called another meeting.

"Officers, things are getting quite out of hand, from what I hear. We gotta show the public that we are doing something. I want you to start arresting people, for anything at all. Just try to bring in a dozen or so this week. I'll call the media and let them know that we're not sitting idle. We asked for a pay hike and we got it. We complained about vehicles and each of you have a brand new Toyota Land Cruiser. You have new uniforms, free lodging, free food. Let's try to get some work done in this place for once and for all," he tried to fire them up.

"I know that none of you, and I'm speaking to Officer Bozo, Officer McLoud, Officer Quail, Officers Piggott and Bum Fatt, ain't got it together to handle no murders and kidnapping. But please officers, show some signs of responsibility and come up with something to go on the papers."

The pep talk shot up their adrenalin and they went out crime busting with full force. They also had to work out to slow down the effects of fast foods. A vengeance against criminals flowed in their blood. Energy from all day eating and drinking had to be channeled into something, before it destroyed them. Also it was the only way to get Yubeedam off their backs.

'Operation Anaconda' was thereby launched and publicized in banners, on the TV, radio and newspapers. A week after, the press was flooded with related headlines.

On Monday it was : Man Arrested for Larceny. The story was that a man was arrested for picking a fruit from a tree on government-owned property. On Tuesday the big broadcast was that a boy was held for urinating on public lands. Wednesday's news was that a woman was held for shoplifting bread. Thursday, an old lady was taken for questioning for illegally selling water on the street; Friday an old man was jailed for driving too slow, and it went on like that for a few more days.

"Great work! I know you all can work hard when you want to," congratulated the chief. "Now they can't accuse us of getting paid for nothing," he flattered his team on their success. "The murders and kidnapping are going on, but that is not our fault. We are doing everything we possibly can under the circumstances."

So, while the public reeled and bawled for murder, the mongoose gang resumed cards, coffee-drinking and merry-making.

Next morning Sergeant Bozo noticed in the paper reports of citizens protesting about that this 'Anaconda' was just ballyhoo, a show meant to pull the wool over their eyes, and that helpless citizens were being harassed by police. A couple was kidnapped, a girl was missing and Anaconda's lips were sealed as usual.

McLoud addressed the press next day.

"We are doing everything in our power to solve these crimes. We ask the public to bear with us as we continue to mount investigations. We have sent out search dogs everywhere to locate bodies if the victims have been killed. So we ask their loved ones to be patient until we locate whatever evidence there is."

Later that evening, Quail asked, "But shouldn't someone have gone out to manage the dogs"

"No need to," answered the super. "That's why they have been trained. By the way, it's almost seven P.M. and they haven't yet returned. I hope they were not stolen!" he exclaimed with concern.

Next morning early, Quail and Bozo were sent out to search for the search dogs, "before someone steals them," worried the boss. Bum Fatt was commanded to put up coffee as usual. "McLoud and Piggot, remain on duty. The press will be here today to ask questions. Relatives will show up for briefings. Me and the constabless have to go out in a while. I'm driving her to the dentist." Then he dismissed himself to collect the coffee pot.

"But boss, you are the one who should be talking to the press," answered Piggott.

"Just give me a break. Okay? I have to drive out a lady this morning," was his hot reply.

A relative of a victim came in to complain.

"You people are having a ball, while our family members are disappearing, and no one gives a damn."

"Constable McLoud, please come and take care of this lady. I didn't sleep too well last night, and I'm getting ready to go out. McLoud! ... Where in the hell is he?"

"Taking a nap, boss," answered Piggott.

"So then, you attend to her," yelled the boss.

The sergeant spun out some mumbo-jumbo that he had heard the day before, about the search dogs, and that two officers had even gone out to search for the search dogs.

" Well I never — searching for search dogs? You people are clearly standing on your heads," exclaimed the astounded woman, breathlessly. "Someone is missing; you do no investigation whatsoever, or try to find them alive, and then you send out dogs to find the dead body. This is beyond belief."

"We are simply acting under orders and doing our best madam. We can't create bodies if there ain't none. We can only ensure that there were killings when the dogs find bodies. We sympathize with your plight, but our hands are tied right now till the dogs come in with their report," was his apologetic answer.

Again the media flashed a range of grievances by concerned citizens against the superintendent and his disgusting police force, but Yubeedam didn't give a damn.

The governor of the state was a second cousin of the

superintendent, so no one had the power to check the nonsense that was going on. One day, however, the governor came to report that his wife was missing and asked if they were doing anything about it.

Nobody at that division had heard about this latest turn of events. The officers, of course, were all busy doing their own thing. McLoud was cursing someone on the phone, Quail was in bed, Bum Fatt was serving coffee, Bozo was watching TV, and the head of the tragedy of errors was in his private chambers, with his female friend.

The governor walked into the chief's room, speechless with horror, but he managed to say in a voice low with anger, "From today on you and your cronies will go on the street. Leave this place at once. I've had it to the brim of my head with complaints against you!"

"But I am doing my job, cousin," answered Yubeedam. He called: "Bozo, Quail, McLoud and you others, get moving. The governor is very angry. Take out ten search dogs. His old lady is missing. We must find the body immediately."

"No, I want you and these loonies to vacate this station. Vacation is over, and I'm giving you an hour to clear out."

So the wacky clan had to leave and the station remained unmanned for a while. But the dogs were the ones in charge then. From that time on, crimes took a plunge somehow, and every one went about their business without fear. Criminals must have heard about the removal of Yubeedam and his circle of clowns.

This bunch ended up in the doghouse, for no one would

give them jobs with the reputations they had. So they hung round the precinct and ate dog-scraps for their meals. And the head dog would bark: " Roff roff! Come get your food, damn boss."

They would run in and eat up, for no one else was kind enough even to give them food. So they prayed that the dogs remained in charge, at least to ensure their daily meals. And the media celebrated the end of the reign of Yubeedam and his staff of sponges.

Air Traffic Control

> "Fart is an excess breeze
> It travels forty degrees
> It kills all the bugs and fleas
> And gives your backside an ease"

This was the jingle that played on radio stations announcing the one and only fartologist in the land, who set up business in a mall.

How he ended up in this location is worth telling. The only training he had was personal experience, and he was hell-bent on turning it into a living by hook or crook.

He first applied for a locale in the Dolphin's Mall in Miami.

"I am a certified fartologist, and I would like to rent a space to open an office."

"Be off with you!" exclaimed the leasing manager. "How dare you think of coming to our mall to operate such a disgusting business? You should rent an open space on the beach. Do you know that you could poison our shoppers with those pungent fumes? You certainly should not be indoors!"

The undaunted doctor knew that malls hosted the greatest traffic of spending folks, and it was highly accessible with parking. So he was determined to ply his trade within one.

Next, he approached the Aventura Mall, which was heavily patronized by rich folks — mostly Latinos from the area, whose favorite staple is rice and beans.

The opportunistic doctor once more approached the leasing manager.

"I am pathologist Dr. Norman Gomez, and I am interested in renting an office here."

The doctor had a heavy upper lip which he took advantage of to twist the sound of the word fartologist to pathologist, to make sure that he wasn't refused this time.

"Okey dokey," replied the cool sales manager. "Just fill in this application and bring in a check for three thousand for the first month's rent."

It was done and the doc put an extra one thousand in an envelope and slipped it into the manager's hand as an act of goodwill, to gain his ongoing support.

Unfortunately, or fortunately, the office was situated near the food court, and his commercial rang on the radio day and night. His office was packed with people of all sizes and shapes. The sign on his door revealed only his name Norman Gomez and his office number. But inside his credentials were advertised in a large poster on the wall :

DR. NORMAN GOMEZ FARTBUSTER
and
AIR TRAFFIC CONTROLLER

**We specialize in treating the following types
of disturbances:**

Silencers

Tremblers

Thunderbolts

Atom bombs

Stink Bombs

Squeakers

The words UP YOUR GAS were written on a logo with an upward pointing finger.

And the farting Latinos provided good business. Arroz and habichuela was the culprit that set the dreaded disease into gear. Those who favored just plain habichuela con dulce, also fell into the notorious farting habit, though their emission had a sweeter fragrance. This latter delicacy is a sweet soup made of kidney beans, sugar, and coconut milk.

Those whose staple food was mofongo, platano or bacalao did not fall victim of the illness, since these foods are more compact and discourage the entry of air into the stomach. Taco Bellyans, too, were also fortunate, because their sandwiches contained less air bubbles.

So the doctor's business did quite well while that of the food court diminished.

A patient suffering from the Silencer came in.

"Doctor, yo tengo this condition which embarrasses me at work. I hear no sound, but the smell vexes everyone around."

"Demonstrate !" ordered the doctor.

And within that instant, pizzas, burgers and tacos were dropped by hands already at the entrance of mouths. The smell of rotten beans filled the mall, which emptied instantaneously.

"Well *Gas X* would solve that problem," he said. "The best way to deal with your co-workers is this: just before the air is released, you must announce that you smell something like a gas leak and act very concerned. In this way, you will escape suspicion. No need to stop eating rice and beans now. Just take the *Gas X* with all your meals."

Another patient complained: "Doctor, I feel my behind tremblando as the fart comes out, and everyone notices. It looks as if a goose is flying out my tail."

"Demonstrate!"

This patient was a lover of spaghetti which creates spaces within the rumble itself.

"Well keep your cellular in your back pocket. Get one of those that vibrates when you get a call. Just take it out whenever the problem occurs and fake a conversation as if your wife is calling you or something. Now, I always give my patients *Gas X*, and you can buy a month's supply to start off. That will take care of the problem. It will be one hundred for my fee and one hundred for the tablets. So for only two hundred a month you will be fine," was the counsel that the doctor gave.

Most of the clients did not realize that the *Gas X* was available at every pharmacy. So they had to resort to Dr. Gomez and his bag of tricks.

Some of the offensive vapors were sweet and some were sour, and many smelled like a latrine. And Dr. Gomez in his white coat, using a special lens, examined the evidence that was blown unto litmus paper every time he said ``demonstrate."

"Dr. Gomez, I think I should be diagnosed with the Thunderbolt."

Now this patient happened to be a Cuban dressed in a bomber jacket, and he weighed about three hundred pounds. He was floating around like a hot air balloon, with a load of arroz, habichuelita, pollito criollo, repollo, done with lots of ajo and cebolla.

"I am ashamed to say that I amaze people with my enfermedad. On a hot sunny day, they hear cracks of thunder, and I hate for them to know that it comes from my very own butt. Sometimes it stinks, sometimes not. He was lying; his puffs of air always stank.

"Demonstrate!" The doctor held the litmus paper close to the site of the explosion, ready to do his hanky-panky.

Prap a tap a tap brap a rap pap a tap! Even the food court eaters heard those peals of thunder, and the fetor that was simultaneously issued drove them out in packs.

The portly hombre had wanted to make a point of the seriousness of his malady, so he pulled off his pants to spotlight the gassy occasion.

"Now *Gas X* is the cure for you," the doctor prescribed. "Of course you should also think of opening a gas station," he joked. "Now a farter must be skilled in the art of deceit. And he must learn how to throw the blame on others. Have you ever thought of that?"

"I am aware, doctor, but my skills are not too sharp. What do you advise?"

"Did you ever wish you were a magician when you were growing up?"

"Si, I thought about it"

"Well this is your chance. You buy a portable disco flasher, and switch it on it to follow up the thunder and create your own lightening, ... very discreetly."

"Sounds bueno, Doc. Now why didn't I think of that?"

"However, amigo, with my *Gas X* the breezes will clear away. You will need to take it for a while, but it should not become a lifetime habit."

A lady named Fatima zigzagged in to be cured, was given her doses of *Gas X*, and went away happily.

Those who were affected by consuming too much Pepsi and popcorn got a special cheap rate from this respectable doctor of gallimaufry.

The *Gas X* was surplus that he bought by the pallets from those companies that sell Aspirin, Mylanta, Tylenol and other drugs that are approaching the expiration date.

And "demonstrate" was his way of putting the customers at ease and proving his expertise in diagnosing the fart.

And a courteous "Gracious, Dios te bendiga" always followed the demonstration.

By now the food court had to shut down and Dr. Gomez's business peaked. His reputation grew and so did his mountain of money.

After a few years of inhaling the putrid fumes, he finally came down with lung cancer. The different types of farts evaluated were mostly based on Arroz and habichuela menus ... Vegetarian, Lacto-vegetarian, Fast food, Cuban, and Mexican Chilly.

But he had enough money to pay for a lung transplant with extra to live on. He was forced to give up practice, though. He, of course, took welfare on the side, for a little extra financial cushioning.

The food court business once more went into full swing, and the leasing manager could not tell why businesses were rising and falling like a seesaw.

The moral of the story here is that arroz and habichuela, whether sweet, sour, or salty, will make you a victim of excess breeze, and you will be forced to visit quackish sharks like Dr. Norman Gomez.

The Fitting Assistant

A lustful man, who had been hooked on the supplement horny goat weed, was looking for employment when he spotted on the internet that *Victoria's Secret* had openings for managers.

So he went for an interview and was appointed to oversee an outlet in Miami.

Women of all ages and classes crowded the store from morning to night, searching for breast enhancing bras, waist tightening panties, thongs, shorts, pajamas, or any other piece of clothing that would give them sexy looks and confidence. All day long, they picked at underwear like hungry chickens.

The goatish manager was thrilled and his eyes traveled all over his head, his tongue dripped, and he resisted blinking as much as possible.

He took not even lunchtime or break time, because his job was more exciting than a roller coaster ride. His eyes bulged and he luxuriated in the middle of a store full of women fidgeting lingerie.

He conceived of a new little duty for himself — fitting

assistant. He would help the women choose the right color, style, and size!

He posted himself outside the trying room, wearing a badge that read Fitting Assistant. Customers were concerned, of course, that they should not buy a bra that was too large, or slack thongs that showed above the waist of the jeans. His extra service was a welcome addition.

The fitting assistant calmed his clients worries. He was cautious not to touch any of them in case they sued him for sexual molestation. So, he worked with his eyes alone.

"And how do these thongs look?" many would ask.

"Oh, you need to buy a larger size. Those look almost invisible on you," he sometimes had to answer.

"And these bras?"

"More padding needed. Your small breasts need the extra lift," was one of his answers.

His job grew more and more fulfilling every day, though he received no extra pay for the self-appointed job. And he kept his hands in his pockets to keep them out of harm's way.

"No, not that nightie — too long. And the blue is too cool. Get the red one. It goes better with you!" He charmed the ladies who were pleased that someone noticed their sexuality.

The store sold T shirts, and he always recommended the ones with the plunging necklines "to keep cooler."

That branch of the chain led all the rest in sales, and the manager's hands shook till they almost fell off. His pay doubled, and he won the annual prize for best employee in the entire company.

As he gained recognition, he became more confident and relaxed on the job, and carried his service to a higher level. He added some new touches.

He now started buckling bras, always on the last hook. "Tighter fit," he told them. Many dames need someone if the fasteners are behind. Little by little his hands became looser and he volunteered to buckle hooks located in the front "so that your new nails will not chip."

His fresh hands would 'accidentally' rub breasts time and time again, but he always sweetened up the clients with words like 'you, of all persons don't need push up bras at all.' Or, he would sometimes excuse himself by saying that he was suffering from palsy in the hands and ask if they could excuse the inconvenience. Then they would blush and overlook the accident.

As his hands became looser his words followed: "Your breasts should be at this level" and he pushed the bust up with both hands to show them exactly where. Or, "those thongs could sit a little bit lower — like here," and the patted the buttocks to show them where.

By and by his hands slid lower and got braver until they approached the vicinity of the promised land. He assigned a salacious clerk, whom he caressed on the bottom as payment whenever he passed her way, to help him with management duties.

His touches grew firmer and stronger. "You need more cleavage here," he would say and push the breasts together. "And you should try some glitter here," pressing his hands on the spot to show them where.

"Here needs to be shaved." He rubbed the bikini line that girls normally shave to go to the beach.

And his touches turned into massages and pinches till his head was no longer in control and he even started to kiss the objects of his desires and asked their owners for their telephones and addresses should they want more.

So complaints started coming in, because the manager had taken his job too far, and women became wildly suspicious of him, although many of them enjoyed the attention when it was given.

The outcry reached the head of the chain, who could think of no other solution than to ship him off to manage another branch in Mexico before lawsuits were filed, because but for his little fault, he was responsible for a ton of revenue not long before.

And he was seen no more at the Miami branch, and everyone, except the wanton clerk of course, celebrated the happy riddance and thought that he was gone for good.

Little did they suspect that he was operating once again in Mexico as manager/fitting assistant.

The bottom line of this paradox is that somewhere at the top of the VS enterprise happened to be an ex-cardinal, the former Holy Father Sinbad, who knew from long experience how to cover up scandal before the '—' hits the fan.

The Powdermilk Cow

"A cow just landed on the moon
To buy a bowl of chowder.
Behind her flew a little spoon
Which turned her milk to powder."

Once upon a time there lived a powdered-milk cow. Yes,
she lived under conditions which would have killed any other.
 It seems strange that a cow should give powdered milk. But
you see, in the sky just above her head, there was a hole in the
ozone layer which prevented even a drop of rain from falling
on that spot — so all the milk she gave was dry.

Also, how did she get her grass? Well the mystery was that
it was truck borne. Yes, it was. A good Samaritan named Sam
Rattan would deliver her a load every week, right in front of
her cud. How she ended up in such a god-forsaken place God
alone knows. It seemed that she hadn't even liquid blood
circulating in her body to mobilize her. If she couldn't make it
on all fours, she would move on all threes to go to the
bathroom, or whenever there was a need that pressured her to
take physical action.

Every day she milked herself because Sam was too busy. He ran a small transport service and in his spare time which was three quarters of the day, he took grass to other animals who shared a similar misfortune. So the powdered milk piled up into mountains. The wind took some away and the rest formed white, rocky hills. The cow (it was a she) fell into a state of worry. Without this factor one cannot be called female. Depression, worry, and female are birds of a feather — they flock together.

"What wastage," she moaned, "that this fine *cintamani* milk cannot even go to the dogs. After so much trouble to make it, it flies away like dust in the wind." She lamented like this for days until a plan landed on her head. A plan not a plane, and it was so brilliant that she was forced to use it so that Sam would not be dazzled whenever he dropped in.

Now Daisy, as we must call her, for it rhymes with Hazy, went to sleep on the plan for seven days and seven nights, because these were the lucky numbers God used to create. The plan was now well compressed and ready to be executed. After that holy week, ambition and money became the controlling forces in the head of the bovine woman.

"The first damn thing we need around here is a fwidge," she mooed. Moorish was her main tongue. "I will sell flavored milkshakes, and milk sweets." The thought of bossing around herself and Sam was so tempting.

So the Samaritan was hired free of charge, to transport the PMC into town to choose a refrigerator. She picked out the commercial type which is used in restaurants. "It's only thwee thousand?" she asked. "I'll take the large one. I will need lots of water for the shakes. Sam Sahib, would you be kind enough to dwop off each week a few bawels of H2O. Can you put it on my cwedit till I start making money to pay you back? Also, please pick up a case each of Vanilla and Chocolate sywup at Food Club. Of course that will also be added to the amount that I owe you. It's just until the cash come wolling in. Don't wowy, your money is safe in my hands."

Once more the Samaritan fell into the trap of helping out a poor dame in distress, and the title *sahib* succeeded in squeezing more goodness out of him. The kind deed got done without too much ado.

The shake factory took shape. Drinks were prepared, boxed or bottled and packed in the refrigerator.

Now our PMC possessed not a single piece of equipment to manufacture the drinks. Did she care about that in the least? Well certainly not. Necessity, being the mother of invention, whispered the solution into her ear, and no doubt she carried it out to a T. She would swallow a few gallons of water, flavoring and milk powder and jiggle around like she was doing the Bamba till the ingredients were mixed better than the best Osteriser shook shake. An extra bit of gargling and then the smooth creamy emulsion would be spat out, packaged, and chilled, for it was warm after leaving the stomach factory.

There were of course the chocolate flavor and the vanilla flavor. Her creative side inspired her to introduce a beverage named Choca Cola. She figured this would compete with the famous Coca Cola. Intuition once more dictated the method — an extra cup of powdered milk would be added to make the mixture thick enough to cause her to choke during production phase. The choked slush would be coughed up and marketed as Choca Cola. This Choca Cola would be sipped through macaroni, since it was too thick to be pulled through plastic straws.

Milk sweets were made by chewing powdered milk and water together. Yes sir, she had the power to chew even water. The gobs were then formed into slabs, put in the sun to dry, and then chopped into squares and stored. You see the cow belonged to the *kamadhenu* caste, a breed that had the power to create anything it desired.

Actually, all cows receive protection in the Cow World, but according to the tale, this lubberly lass broke loose from the rest of the herd while they were grazing on a mountain peak, and braps — she fell down into a valley of the shadow of death called Earth, where cows are murdered for food every day by the millions. This report is taken from *Tittle Tattle Archive*, Vol 7, entitled "Planet Of Pure Cows."

Now, that handy gray matter called brain was conspicuous by its absence in the poor thing. It seems that this good substance had bidden her farewell long before she was conceived. Not even did a sprinkling of horse sense visit her even once in a blue moon, and so she thought not of where her patrons would come from, which helped contribute to the distressing fact that she had none.

The Samaritan then took another main role in the show — special customer number one. The PMC took care to make him sign 'cwedit slips,' whenever he had no change to pay for the milkshakes or sweets, and she let him know that she was doing him a favor by trusting him with 'victuals.' In fact, for emphasis, she had him hang a banner across the shop that announced IN GOD WE TRUST, OTHERS CASH.

The fridge was brimming to the max, and the PMC and Sam were the only two eaters in sight. Hungry ants, who tried to squeeze in to savor some of the goodies, were hastily sprayed with Hot Shot.

The PMC herself began putting away a massive portion of the delights in her stomach, to make room for upcoming productions (although the poor ants lost their life just for smelling the goods). The powdered milk was not going to blow away again. At least that waste had stopped, and Sam was once more ordered to hang another banner with the wise saying WASTE NOT, WANT NOT, SAID THE OLD LADY WITH THE THIN WAIST. The PMC's abdomen which was clearly wasted, because of not following this rule, opposed the meaning of the word thin.

Slowly, a new idea started bubbling in her head. It was known that bullshit was full of antiseptic qualities, and what better way to put it to use than to sell it? So once more the Samaritan busied himself displaying a huge banderole which read VACA CACA FOR SALE. And the cow waited for buyers, who might have well been disembodied.

You see, the intake of shakes, toffees, and hay was transformed into tall dung heaps, which was also a potential money puller according to her logic. She thought the caca would also be auntie septic, since it came from the body of a female. And Sam was recruited to build a shed to store the goods (as if there was anyone else in sight to do the bidding of a holy cow) for he actually could see a divine halo over her head

A few months passed and no money came in, for there was none spilling in the neighborhood. Bills piled up, and the interest on the fridge was fifty dollars a month. The Samaritan did not send in any bills for his services, because this was not the way friends dealt. Contracts were signed only by the lips, as usual, even though that sort of agreement usually shortens the term of the friendship by ninety-five percent.

Instead of throwing away the bill paper, the cow utilized it as wrapping for the Vaca Caca. Remember the sign — Waste Not; Want Not. She also reasoned that since the heat was sizzling, they were located somewhere close to that Mexican border, where Latinos were always trying to smuggle in.

So the chocolate shakes were pulled down from the shelves and relabeled Chocolatina and Chocolatino, male and female.

The hole in the ozone layer widened because of the gas released by the refrigerator, and Sam the handyman was ordered to put the fridge at a lower temperature, when he dropped by one day, to bring a load of grass. The goodness of his heart prevented him from realizing that the hallowed one saw him as nothing but a tool to be used, reused and abused, for the sake of her kooky plans.

And once more Sam was called to duty. Another banner reading FREE MACARENA SHOW FOR NINOS had to be painted and hung. The Macarena dance was to be incorporated with the blending of the drinks. In other words blending and dancing were fused into one act for the show. A jukebox arrived to provide the music, and it appeared in the shop compliments of Sam who was always anxious to do a good deed with his credit card. It cost only two thousand, but money

would be soon be rolling in the cow assured him, and he
believed it because he liked her — he was beginning to think
like his thick-witted friend.

His payments were made because his trucking business
scraped in a little revenue. The lesser debts which the PMC
owed him for services, the flavors, and other things, caused
him shame to mention them. His faith in her promises
remained blind.

But the dim-sighted cow had no way to pay hers, till
finally the refrigerator payments plus the interest hit the five
thousand line. That was when bullshit hit the ceiling. The
animal became so habituated to the ice cold drinks that she
rejected the thought of returning the fridge.

One day another brilliant idea struck the cow like a
thunderbolt — "What if I sell myself to McDonald's for five
thousand, in this way I won't have to weturn the fwidge." She
could not conceive of life without Mr. Fridge, her new live-in
love, but her head was too sloppy to realize that she would be
dead after the sale.

And therefore McDonald's truck came one Saturday day
morning to collect its burger material, and the PMC bade
sayonara to Sam Sahib, but not to her beloved fridge. "No
pwoblem man," she mooed , with a slick grin as she climbed
aboard the truck — and the fridge was saved.

The moral here is that death and debt are relatives —
synonyms even. Light bulb bright ideas are usually the
floppiest. Sometimes it is better to let sleeping dogs lie, or
powdered hills blow away in the wind. And lastly, a Samaritan
loses his worth if he poses as sitting duck for an ambitious

162
ignoramus.

The Seller

A street Jew, after trying his hand at different professions, decided to return to vending. It seemed quite a gainful and decent way to make a living. So he set up his operations in different fairs and malls.

And trade expanded. There was a breed of unstable money flying around — the type desperate to leave its owner's company at any cost. So, it always sought a way to move on, and the seller was always around, with his hands cupped open, to catch it when it flew.

He sold gold-filled as gold and stainless steel as silver. Even a stamp saying 325 which means nothing was printed on the inside of silver-looking jewelry, so that when buyers squinted their eyes like the Chinese, looking for the 925 signature that usually confirms sterling silver, their eyes would become so sore trying to read it that they would give up and buy the damned thing anyway. Loaded pockets itched to dispose of their burdens, which was thence offloaded on the pleased seller.

"Is this gold or silver?" asked the wild, foggy-headed shoppers.

"Oh, that is gold with a silver vermeil," he would say.

"And how much you are asking?"

"Only one hundred today."

And a hundred would be fished out and handed over for a stainless steel bracelet.

Plastic and resin would be marketed as amber.

"And what are these lines on the stone?"

"Oh, those are not defects. They are the natural streaks of the amber."

"And how much do you ask?"

"Only one hundred and twenty, and it is set in sterling silver, as you can see."

And eager hands pulled out eager notes, gained by blood, sweat, and tears, and passed them over to the glib peddler in exchange for a hunk of brown resin.

But this is the nature of business — lies are its main stronghold, and fast talk is its mag wheel. Since it is uncensored and legal, the unglib and unsharp, who make up the consumer populace, illusion themselves by thinking that they are getting a great deal for their money.

The true value of an item is not its market value — the latter is created by merchants and supply coupled with demand. But who knows or cares what the real value is? These factors are carefully guarded from the buyer's knowledge.

Government is the biggest con-artist on the scene. A lifetime is spent paying a mortgage for a house worth only a few years of salary.

This is the harsh reality that faces us. But there seems to be no remedy in sight.

A person becomes a slave for life, paying for a little shelter and a few amenities, because of ignorance of real value, and pressure from every direction claiming that this is the way it should be.

So the huckster made up his mind to strike while the iron was hot, (as if it ever gets cold). He got into real estate. He bought land, built houses, and sold them at one percent less interest than his competitors. He even bought swampland and marketed it as residential lots.

In the meantime, the buying masses were too busy attending school to learn a profession, so that they could spend their lifetimes paying for housing, food and other necessities. They were too busy as well to ponder what the real value of life is or what they should really be doing with their precious time.

So they became the sacrificial lambs that fell into the hawker's trap, and he hopscotched around in many business enterprises with monstrous success.

He sold real estate, housewares, vacations and even grave plots. And vendees lined up to bestow their lifetime's worth on him.

Sometimes their cautious side would present itself, for though they were decorated with diplomas, it seemed that their wits would leave on wool-gathering trips, for extremely long periods.

Whenever their wits returned, they would haggle over a fifty cent discount on a pair of sunglasses, or buy the fake ones never minding that they were paying interests of over one hundred thousand on their homes.

And the Jew observed their worry and tried to please all of them with love and care, for they represented his bread, butter, and grand estate.

Some of the smartened ones would come to his booths in the malls to fight over prices, for he still kept the shops running.

So he would sell cheap to satisfy them. If they wanted silver for five dollars, he would give it to them and if they wanted it cheaper, he would go still lower on the price — he invented the *Priceline* concept, though some other trickster came later and claimed the idea to be his. The strategy now was to always to keep the patrons coming back to him.

"Is this bracelet twenty-two carat gold?" some buyer would ask.

"It certainly is," would be the answer — a true one.

" And what is the price?"

"Only one hundred dollars."

Bang! The bracelet would be slammed down so hard and the angry client would walk away. And the Jew would call out begging, "Come back, come back! I will give it for fifty." And he made the sale. And he would even give lagniappe with the sale. He reasoned that when he sold a Trump apartment, for which he was an agent, he would walk away with the humongous catch.

Big and small fishes, red herrings as well as blue ones, trout and salmon, were all fed bait, and they crowded into his net, were caught, and hauled home to be eaten, while they were innocently swimming across the Lake of Survival. The monger and his government friends celebrated, and they achieved in an hour what the suckers took two lifetimes to do.

> So the vendor sold and the vendee bought;
> The former stored gold and the latter naught.
> Senators and congressmen feted with abandon,
> As bankers and brokers hid fortunes in London.
> And consumers purchased with such reckless delight
> That concerned onlookers worried for their plight.
> The credit companies stacked wealth to the ceiling.
> And debtors were left to resort to stealing.
> Sportsmen, singers, and actors pulled in the most cash
> And their government friends supported the bash.
> While the masses slaved for house and entertainment,
> Those running the show plotted their arraignment.
> Old folks late with taxes that they couldn't afford
> Would be thrown in the slammer for taxation fraud.
> One of the things that causes vexation
> Is when they seize your property for tax evasion.
> It now seems impossible to clean up this mess.
> To clean up the mess! To clean up the mess!

So the story goes, that the peddler and the peddlees continued business together, until the end, for none of them will see the light that shines at the end of the tunnel, because there is none.

And this is why consumers remain blind and gullible as of this date, with a constant itch biting their fingertips ... Spend! Spend! Spend!

Vegetarian Delights

Once a world-renowned master set up an ashram and recruited boys and girls to go out and distribute the message through books. These boys and girls were actually grown ups but the label was somehow coined. Their breakfast menu was rice, yellow lentil soup, curried vegetables, flat bread, and a sweet farina pudding known as *halvah*.

The enlistees woke at four am. for worship and meditated until seven, at which time there was a lecture. Then the meal was served, as they sat on the floor and ate with their hands off of steel plates. A mountain of steaming rice was established on each plate, by a designated food server. The boiling hot yellow pea soup was ladled into a crater on top of the rice, to form a spicy lake. The curry, bread and *halvah* soon joined the assembly, as they were dropped around the mountain's sides. It was a nice hot breakfast to start any day, but being spooned out at a regularity of three hundred and sixty five days a year, it was enough to make the recipients hallucinate about something lighter like milk and cereal.

After the load was shoveled into the stomachs, with some chewing involved, the trainees were expected to immediately go out and spread the word. And some of these abdomens were built to accommodate only half the amount that was forced down. Now that the worshipers were ready to hit the road, they were piled into windowless, cargo vans without seats, and ferried off to do the pick. Vehicles were packed in the described fashion every morning.

Fifteen men stuffed to the neck, with a spicy disorder of Indian muddle, crammed in the back of a goods van with books, were on their way to do their sacred work. Now this heavy bill of fare was enough to invoke an hour or two of deep slumber, but our book champions were not allowed such a delicious luxury.

Instead they tumbled, rolled, and back flipped over each other, as the lorry braked, bent corners and raced to get them on the site early enough to do a full day of God's work. Sometimes the food would try to escape through their throats; sometimes through their hindquarters. But the passage was certainly rocky, a steamy van-load of jumbled missionaries, with a brew of flavors almost spilling out of their guts, fortunate enough not to macerate in the fleshy stew.

Some of them were lucky to have cushions, while others were not so lucky; their rumps and bones scraped the steel floors of the vehicles, for they were not carpeted. "*Prabhu,* please go slower," complained some of the passengers, whose bellies were exploding with curry, but the *prabhu* was too worried about not reaching on time to pay them any heed.

"*Prabhu,* please drop me here," and one of the riders disembarked and walked through mangroves, tall bushes and even swam across a river to get to the location, for he could not endure the torture of the rough journey.

Every morning the mission vans rolled, and unknown to the world, their occupants capsized in the back, with abdominal inter-fusions. All the world saw them on street corners, giving out books for donations, but no one knew of the behind-the-scenes happenings.

The heat and darkness contributed to the misery of the ride, but the volunteers considered themselves fortunate to be handpicked by God for this divine occupation. It was the sacrifice that was required to help others. The next meal would be eaten when they returned to the *ashram* at night— so the morning intake of fuel for their jobs was designed to last till then. After a hard day's work they came back weary and sat down to dinner, which was another noteworthy affair.

A rice and lentil mixture displayed fried sesame bread-sticks sticking out at the top, like yellow ribbons awaiting the arrival of a loved one, possibly intended to whet appetites. Now the food sharer did not have the patience to wait on them in the evening, so he would dish out a plateful for each, and leave it uncovered for the starved book-pushers to feast on. Unfortunately, we the public are hot to criticize religious workers, but these unsung people sometimes bear inhumane hardships to share their blessings with us, and it's commendable, actually.

So this nightly dinner was a chilled plate that sat out for about an hour, and it iced the stomach as the night grew colder. And if you were asthmatic, crapaud smoked your pipe.

Fathers, mothers, and siblings tried to reclaim their relatives from this austere lifestyle with words like: "You are not an ashramite; you're an ass-ramite." But that made no impact on the chosen ones.

They looked forward to a special love feast on Sundays. Prospective followers who were rounded up on the field were invited to this bash. At the same time, the interacting preachers would have the chance to tutor them further on spiritual practices. This love feast referred to a grand vegetarian banquet which was served around six pm.

Different courses were spooned into cellophane thin paper plates, for guests and hosts alike. It was the most delightful day of the week for the preachers. Every dish was ladled either on top, below, on the side or in the middle of the next. A muddle-some merger arose, comprised of treats like yellow raisin rice, fiery hot apple chutney, icy almond milk pudding thickened with rice, vegetables stewed in hot spices and turmeric, fried whole wheat sesame breads, blazing *sambars*, sour yogurt, sweet farina *halvah*, and powdered milk balls fried and served soaked in a thick syrup. This was to be washed down with lemonade made from lemon powder. The liquids from the exotic merger soaked and melted the paper thin plates, which were disturbingly inadequate, for leaks and splutters swished here and there causing annoyance.

If these preparations made it down to the eater's stomach, they would be pleading with him or her to rush home and lie down, for the diversity of the medley soon proved indigestible, once it hit chest level. On the jerky drive, the gourmand would be tempted to park just anywhere and rest a bit, to settle the troublesome clutter which tormented the core of the thorax and guts. The sweet cold milk pudding combined with the fiery fruit chutney was enough to do the trick, not to speak of

the dozen of assorted flavors which rallied around them.
 Fortunate were the predicants who were home-based, for if
the toilet called, they would not have to run very far. These
were appointed to wash and clean up after the eat out, and
they stumbled around with heavy bellies carrying out their
chores, while expecting, but not hoping for the call of nature.

Another element of the love feast was the food-line. Now,
orderliness was required so that everyone could get an even
share. Previous occasions of pushing, elbowing, yelling, and
bribing proved to be unfair to the shier bunch. So the line was
a rule that could not be overstepped; otherwise servers would
pretend to go on strike until order returned.

This file, stretching for what seemed like a half mile,
crawled slowly as a snake, toward the banquet table, to taste
tantalizing vegetarian delights. Everyone was aware of the
danger that sometimes the most desirable eats like milk balls
or *samosa* would run out, and that brought immense stress to
those way in the back. The anxiety was so great, that they
would keep chatting along the way, in an effort to rid
themselves of it, as the queue snailed forward.

The scramble to occupy a place in that line was as furious
as lion wrestling, and each one held on to his position, as if it
were the last drop of life. Those at the back would look ahead,
see people walking off with plates laden with the dozen
merged items, and would wonder, with excruciation, if their
plate would be so diversely packed. So they would hold their
hearts, stomachs and wafer plates in their hands, as the tension
mounted.

Shoulders would drop, faces would sour, when hit by the

stark reality that their merger consisted of a sheer duet — rice and curry vegetables — and a paper cupful of semi-hot lemonade. Internally they would twist in disgust and disappointment, while struggling to maintain a pleasant show of evening *tete-a-tete.*

But it was vegetarian, it was free, and therefore the risk of missing it caused much worry. But those who left unsatisfied were determined to try the next Sunday, with secret plots of how to get ahead in the line, even if it meant missing a section of the weekly lecture, to hover next to the food table, waiting for the word, "go."

And they ate and ate, as if it was the last supper, not caring about the sweet, sour, hot or salty fumes that would rise from their stomachs as the night phased on.

The veggie heads soon hit upon a plan to convert folks to vegetarianism. They would give cooking classes to whomever would pay five dollars per lesson. And the students gathered around to learn. "Well today," the teacher explained, "we will teach you how to make vegetarian pizza." And the class looked on in wonder, for none of them had stretched out their brains enough to figure out the mystery behind the meatless dish. The cooking instructor simply flattened out pizza dough, spread a layer of tomato sauce, a layer of broccoli, covered it with cheese, stuck it in the oven, and exclaimed: "Bingo, you have homemade vegetarian pizza!"

The class could not believe it was so uncomplicated. They stared in amazement, tasted it and praised it to the high heavens — that it was made from natural ingredients, and it would guard them against diseases.

Vegetarian calzones were nothing but calzone dough filled with eggplant and cheese, instead of meat and cheese, and fried.

"Today, we will show you how to make egg-less cake. You will need exactly four settled cups of white flour, a wee touch of salt, four level teaspoons of baking powder, two level teaspoons of baking soda, two sticks of softened butter, a cup of white sugar... Combine all the ingredients with one cup of water. Using a cake beater, mix it like this for five minutes. Then pour it into a greased pan and bake for thirty minutes at three hundred and fifty degrees, like this." As he spoke, the teacher waved his hands like a magician over the batter, and sprinkled the baking powder and soda with a mystic flicker of the fingers.

Now, the educatees could not see that eggs merely had to be omitted to make the healthful cake. The texture was drier, but no one noticed, and they stood up, clapped their hands, and begged for more exclusive recipes.

So the food propagandists and their flock ranted and raved about their vegetarian alternatives. Some of these devotees were so fanatic about animal protection, that they wore no leather in any form: shoe, belt, or handbag. However rennet-filled pizza and cheese dishes managed to find their way down their stomachs as often as once a day.

And the picture of Krishna whom they worshiped, would end up in the rubbish. most of the time. For it was printed on every bit of stamp, label, T Shirt, cheap watch, stationery, incense box, that was temporarily usable and later to be thrown in the garbage. Glossy Krishna calendars were forwarded to the dumping grounds to be mixed with filth when the year changed.

But these vegetarian visionaries meant no wrong. They just worked as they honestly thought best, and they were treated with respect, for they were gentler and humbler than most run of the mill people.

Some of them were fond of *soya*. Everything from ice cream, to bread, to hot dogs, was *soya*-based, so much so that they themselves started to look as fit as walking *soya* beans.

Another activity of this *ashram* was a food for life program. Up for grabs every Saturday morning, around street corners was spicy rice soup and *halvah*. Beggars, the homeless, and rapscallions would fight each other for the spoils, while the food sharers would eat the leftovers.

Sometimes the food workers would approach normal people, to entice them with vegetable fritters named *pakoras*, on a plate. Falling on bended knees and bowing deeply they would say: "Please try a little *pakora*, please, and give a donation, if you like." The *pakoras* would be offered to extended hands. Later the street sweeper would sweep up loads of the fries, which were thrown away in disgust, and the missionaries would cry about the waste. But come next Saturday morning, bright and early they were back on the job: "Please, try a little *pakora*, please."

Vegetarian food, of course, is superior to non-veg, and those who realized this became lifelong plant-based eaters. But members of this jolly cult believed in it to the max, and some of them swallowed so much food that it brimmed in their eyes, ears and noses. And this part is not fiction; it's historical.

They ate their way to salvation and left no stones unturned to facilitate their voracious hobby.

So this merry bunch of preachers lived a life of hardship, but they were paid off by good food.   And they chanted their *mantras*, danced, and hoped and prayed for ten thousand years more to meet them in this state.

*Trinidad cannot produce
one real pundit, samjhe?*

Why Shankar Changed Sides

Everyone comes into this world with a certain mentality. Either you're born with the mind of a politician, that of a teacher, a student, a trader, or just an ordinary worker who does not mind working for the other groups. But it's unavoidable, one must be born with a certain occupational mindset.

At the top of the ladder is the teacher, because it is he who molds the politicians and leaders with his vast expanse of knowledge. It was the priests and religious ministers who controlled the rulers of long ago, and they still have a lot of influence on policies today.

The artist, dancer or prostitute, or anyone selling his talent or products is within the mercantile mode of operations. The majority of people in the world today serve the other classes for money.

A politician's son may not be a politician. A merchant's child might turn out to be a priest. The roles keep changing as the modes of nature reflect differently on each person just like light reflects differently on a prism each time. These days no one is purely one thing. Being born the son of a pastor does not mean you could not wind up being a president. The rules are not very strict. It's all based on how nature affects each person.

You are born to be what you must be regardless of who your parents are. Of course parents try hard to mold you into the lifestyle of their choice, and it works in many cases. But the final result depends on you and the kind of mind you were born with.

We hear so much about the caste system of India. There was a huge outcry from brahmin parents when *dalit* children were granted education privileges, meaning they would sit together in the same classroom with children of higher castes. It's good to protect the values of your birthright. But there are important values like compassion, kindness, humility, faithfulness to what you profess to be and honesty, qualities that should not be sacrificed as you promote the greatness of your own 'tradition.' A humble person with a kind heart is superior to an arrogant member of the elite of high stock.

Shankar was an Indo-Trinidadian whose great grandparents had gone to the island to work in the 1900s in order to escape the hardship of the Indian famine. It was now the 1990s and Shankar was feeling a bit restless, Trinidad being such a small island. He decided to take to traveling, but everywhere he went people called him Indian. However, Indian-born people insisted on calling him Trinidadian.

This confused Shankar a bit. Was he what he thought he was or was he what people saw him as? Shankar came from a pundit family and he practiced Vedic rituals every day. He also performed rites for whoever requested, so he identified more with India than with Trinidad.

One time he went on a holiday to St. Martin. While he was shopping, the Indian merchants began to pound him with questions like: "What is the caste of people in Trinidad?"

"Well they're mixed just like in India or any other part of the world," he tried to answer.

"Are they high caste? We heard that they are low caste?" was the persistent question.

"I can't give a precise reply," said Shankar.

"We come from a very high caste in India," was the response to Shankar's uncertain answer.

That night he sat in a restaurant having his vegetarian meal. Right there before his eyes he saw the 'high caste' traders devouring big plates of meat and gulping down rum by the bottle. They seem to be savoring the goodies like connoisseurs.

Well, thought Shankar, what a world of Jekylls and Hydes. I'm supposed to be a low born westerner, but at least I am a vegetarian.

Shankar's next journey took him to Dominica where he experienced the same kind of bewilderment. Indian business people 'interviewed' him. "Do you speak the Indian language?"

"Somewhat. I am not quite fluent," was his reply, which made him unpopular immediately.

The Indians looked quite disappointed and stopped the conversation. To them he was a creolized *chamar*. He could tell this by their attitude. Of course, the first question they had posed was the caste one. When he told them his family were pundits, they had replied that anyone who could say prayers in Hindi could become a pundit in the Caribbean.

Everywhere he turned he saw the same phenomenon. High caste Indians were flocking to the Caribbean to scoop up dollars.

People from pundit families like his were the ones who had established thousands of temples and centers of yoga and meditation, and they dedicated their existence to this kind of work even till today without any kind of distraction. But Shankar could not find acceptance from any of the Indian caste elites.

On the same island he met one such woman with a close-cut boycott hairstyle that made her look like a man. She had a one inch red paper dot on her forehead.

"Knowing a few *mantras* does not make you high caste," she was talking down to him.

"I am not saying I am a high caste. I am just doing what my father trained me to do and I don't know anything else," Shankar tried to defend himself.

What could he say? He recalled that she was the same person he saw dining in Kentucky Fried as he was passing outside the night before. How dare she take the role to lecture him about caste?

However, he thanked his stars that he was part of a circle of family and friends who were honest to themselves. They did not profess to be too high.

Back home he went. He had to take his child to the

university to sign up for classes. Some Indian artists had come there to sell their trade. There was a *tabla* player who called out the beats of his drum in the voice of a hen. There was a lady who spun around dancing Kathak for two long hours. After the dance she asked for questions. Someone wanted to know if she didn't feel dizzy. So much humiliation for a buck, Shankar thought.

A famous Kapoor actress came to the island to promote herself. As the show ended a fan went up to shake her hand. She protested that she was brahmin stock and could not shake hands with people from off the street.

Shankar was amazed. Was this not the same lady who made love to hundreds of heroes on screen, drank and danced in public? A person who traded flesh wasn't a trader? It confused him so much he could not sleep at night.

One day he bought the local papers. An oil executive from India had been flogged by a pimp. The story was that the man had used the service of a prostitute and was so cheap he did not want to pay the total of the bill. He asked for a discount. The prostitute called her pimp to take care of him and he was beaten unconscious. Strange, thought Shankar, for someone who hailed from India and spoke Hindi.

The next year, he went to New York for his holidays. While there he decided to go to the Indian shops to buy provisions to take home. On stepping off the train in Jackson Heights, he thought he had reached the black hole of Calcutta. The dirt and mountains of garbage piled everywhere like nobody's business hardly left room to walk. Bollywood songs blasted everywhere and the restaurants were filled with people eating and drinking.

"How could I eat food in these conditions?" he wondered. That day he did not eat.

A few days later he took a plane down to Miami to visit a cousin who worked for a prestigious Indian. The cousin related that the man was trying to divorce his wife, because he was dating a twenty-two year old Mexican girl. But, thought Shankar, low born me and my Trinidadian wife are together twenty years, doing prayers everyday. Am I really better than a born Indian?

Shankar decided he must align himself with one side. He had to put an end to his confusion. And that side could well be the non-Indian side. Were not Westerners promoting yoga and meditation selflessly throughout the world? He personally knew scores of them. Shankar considered changing sides.

But maybe, maybe, I am wrong, he thought. I should take more time to sort this out. I must do some more checking before making any decision. Perhaps it's my fault-finding attitude. Shankar was a humble man who got his primary education in a Christian school and he had learned how to be sincere and introspective. He was not a man to act rashly.

His father had always told him about the sacred Ganges river and how important it was to make pilgrimages to India. He decided: "I must make a trip to India in this lifetime."

So he saved for six months and bought the ticket.

On his arrival, his senses went into a state of shock. The first thing he saw was a little baby on the street covered with flies like nobody's business. Perhaps the mother was nearby begging or was the child abandoned? But no one batted an eye as thousands of people marched by. The place was overcrowded with beggars as well as young mothers and children begging for food.

Shankar, when he used to identify with India, used to be proud that NRIs were the richest immigrant group in the USA, making at least eighty thousands dollars per year on average. At least the Indian publications constantly boasted of it. Shankar did not observe an ounce of compassion or charity despite the wealth of the Indian migrants. He was heartbroken to see the conditions of people living in boxes on the streets everywhere.

But these movie stars who make a million dollars per movie must be aware of the situation, he thought. Shankar had also read that Swatch watches that sell for 30,000 dollars each had their biggest market in India. India had the vastest stock of pure gold, and the rich spent millions of dollars on weddings.

Rediff was always boasting that there were so many Indians on the billionaire list, but what was the value, Shankar questioned? All he saw was poverty for miles around, wherever he went, at least for the first week, until he got accustomed to it.

Indian periodicals like to boast of things like one in every three Americans are either black or Asian. What was the sense, Shankar asked himself, if they shared not a penny with their poor brothers and sisters. India's riches must surely be hidden in banks or abroad, he thought, because he saw no sign of it anywhere.

He cried and could not sleep for the first few days. He

made a promise to give a little something to beggars whenever he could. Despite the super-affluence of many Indians, Shankar discovered by talking to a fellow tourist that eighty-six percent of Indians live with two dollars or less a day in wages; forty-four percent live with less than one dollar a day and twenty-five percent had hardly any money for food.

In a few days it was time for him to visit the Ganges and he had to commute for a few hours. Once he reached the location he took rickshaw-bike transport to the river. After some minutes he suddenly found himself in a cloth shop. The shop owner was apparently paying the rickshaw man to bring customers, so Shankar became the latest victim. As much as he protested, the driver would not take him to his destination until he bought something. The clothes were nice so he gave in and purchased.

By this time it was late and Shankar asked the man to take him to a specific hotel for the night. But the man dropped him at another, dingy hotel that was no doubt giving him a commission. Shankar had to wage a war of words which lasted an hour until the rickshaw man agreed to take him to the hotel of his choice.

It was another day of agony for Shankar, but he consoled himself. Tomorrow he would get to see the Ganges.

So early in the morning the next day he hired a rickshaw to take him there. He had rehearsed bowing down and praying at the sight of the holy river. He reached and prepared for the rituals. But suddenly he discovered the worst shock of his life. There was human litter — excrement scattered everywhere on the bank of the holy river.

Shankar refused to believe his eyes and would not look. Gradually his opened his eyes and tried to focus his sight on the river alone as he said his prayers with a lot of anxiety.

I must bathe, he thought, so he tip-toed his way among the mess and proceeded into the Ganges.

There he was filled with peace as he submerged himself for about ten minutes. "Ma," he prayed, "may I always worship you even though I live far away and speak English."

Shankar remembered the red-dot woman who lectured him about caste back on the island. If, only if, she would come and instruct people over here, maybe some of these offenses could be stopped. All these high-ranking people posing as seers and knowers were in the West pursuing money, and here he was faced with this heartbreaking situation. Thinking like this he felt hopeless and shed a few tears.

Some people don't see the pock marks on their own skin. They look for faults everywhere else especially abroad where they judge the situation without understanding. Going to a place with an aura of superiority really backfires and causes shame, as your own faults are discovered by others. Money is the driving force behind all evils and once it becomes the chief goal nothing else matters. Even the most sacred of things gets dumped in the garbage.

For one week Shankar stayed and bathed each day and bore the pain of seeing the holy river desecrated by Indians. I'm not caste enough for them, he thought, but is this the image they are proud to present to the world? Shankar was becoming more and more convinced about giving up any identification with the breed of Indians who harassed him in the West.

It was time to continue his pilgrimage. He set out to the holy towns where he met tourists here and there. One young woman was crying that someone had just grabbed her breast. One of her friends had been raped a few days ago. She was given a drugged ladoo by a 'respectable' person and then assaulted. This can't be real, Shankar thought.

Soon Shankar found himself in a famous temple that was packed with pilgrims. He left his sandals outside which was the custom. He carried a bag which had a recorder and a cheap camera. During the prayers everyone had to bow down for three minutes, so he placed his bag on the floor. When Shankar arose, his bag was gone.

There were some ladies sewing large garlands in an area of the temple room. Shankar noticed that one of them kept digging out ear wax as if she was digging yams with the back of the needle. This place, Shankar thought, needs a lot of high caste people to give lectures. What are they doing in the West judging who was *chamar* and who was *mleccha*? Wasn't the saying "charity begins at home" still valid ?

On leaving the temple he discovered that his shoes were gone. He continued his trek barefooted. If only a few of the migrating upper classes would invest some money to help make changes instead of boasting of how rich they were becoming. Bad image for their country, he thought.

The trip disappointed Shankar in many ways. He boarded for his last train journey which was to last six hours. One person kept his legs on the passenger seat and refused to let the poor man sit. I don't remember seeing this kind of thing back home, thought Shankar.

One of the things he noticed was that the pictures of the gods they worshiped were on every incense box and item of commerce — placed there to make them sell. But wouldn't these things end up in the garbage at some time? At least I am very conscious about it, he thought.

But in the name of money even the most sacred thing goes to the dogs. He became more and more convinced that status and mentality do not have to do with language and where you were born. It is your deeds that make you, nothing else. It was a moment of enlightenment for Shankar, as he concluded his trip to the holy land.

He reached back home, rested and gave a lot of thought to things. Back there some of his countrymen addressed him as an Indian as usual. But now he did not feel pleased; perhaps shame was what he felt.

"West Indian, Trini- Indian is what I am," he answered, each time they called him Indian.

Indian born men and married ladies with big plastic dots on their forehead questioned him about the caste of Indians from Trinidad whenever he traveled to the islands and the US. They asked whether the people were high class or *chamar* and if they spoke Hindi or English. Caste? Caste? caste? was the famous question.

"*Chamar*," became his soft reply, and they would leave him in peace.

Shankar embraced anyone he met that was trying to do good. He didn't give up the religious duties that his father had taught him.

He walked and talked with everyone, teaching and sharing with them how to better the world. He did not feel bad about being asked caste questions, because he was now equipped with realizations.

Finding out that forty million feticides had been performed in India to eliminate the burdensome female sex was too much for him to swallow. Shankar opted to give up any Indian identification he had left and become a citizen of the world.

He wanted to be a human being of kindness and compassion. The heartlessness of caste and rank which he experienced was not the path for him.

In the first few years of the twenty first century, Shankar became fully enlightened about who he was — a humble speck of a world citizen. No more was he confused about his identity. This is the story of the enlightenment of Trinidad pundit Shankar Gosai.

About the Author

Drupadi Singh boils like a curry brew of many different
flavors produced by childhood and current influences: Hindu
rituals and priests, a multi-religious mother, ancestral
grandmothers who recited the Hindi *Ramayana*, a terribly strict
father, calypso, steel bands, rastafarian music and language
paranda. She was schooled under the universities of London
and Cambridge and excelled in fiction-writing. She speaks
West Indian dialect and Spanish. Her uncles would come over
at night and tell stories for fun about *socouyant*, *doen* and
lagahoo, fearsome mythical characters of the Caribbean
underworld. Then they would end the evening playing music
and singing with *dhantal*, *dholak* and harmonium if there was
one.

She did a bit of journalism for the *Express* and then worked
with the Ministry of Industry as a clerk for two years in Port of
Spain. All along she maintained an interest in god and
attended churches of all faiths. At the age of twenty-two she
switched to full time retrospection. She has persisted with her
philosophical pursuits and desires to share her ideas with the
world. She enjoys *salsa*, the philosophy of the Beatles and the
stories of *Bharat Natyam*. She loves to shop in *Marianne*, *Old
Navy* and *Marshalls* for chic fashion bargains, and, of course, to
chill with friends drinking hot *chai* under a banyan or jackfruit
tree, where else but at the nature rich zone of the University of
Puerto Rico, Rio Piedras campus? Drupadi worships nature.
 She regrets that the jackfruit are removed green from the trees
for security reasons. Her fables are for the purpose of
upliftment and amusement. She extends her blessings with
sweetness like the sunshine to one and all.